# FIRST CAME A MURDER

# John Creasey

Master crime fiction writer John Creasey's 562 titles have sold more than 80 million copies in over 25 languages. After enduring 743 rejection slips, the young Creasey's career was kickstarted by winning a newspaper writing competition. He went on to collect multiple honours from The Mystery Writers of America including the Edgar Award for best novel in 1962 and the coveted title of Grand Master in 1969. Creasey's prolific output included 11 different series including Roger West, the Toff, the Baron, Patrick Dawlish, Gideon, Dr Palfrey, and Department Z, published both under his own name and 10 other pseudonyms.

Creasey was born in Surrey in 1908 and, when not travelling extensively, lived between Bournemouth and Salisbury for most of his life. He died in England in 1973.

# THE DEPARTMENT Z SERIES

# FIRST CAME A MURDER

JOHN CREASEY

ipso books

This edition published in 2016 by Ipso Books

First published in Great Britain by Melrose in 1934

Ipso Books is a division of Peters Fraser + Dunlop Ltd

Drury House, 34-43 Russell Street, London WC2B 5HA

# Author's Note

*First Came a Murder* was my fifth book. When it was published in 1935 I was proud of it indeed. Dorothy L. Sayers, then the crime book critic of the *Sunday Times,* injured that pride considerably when she said in her inimitable style: 'Here we have the thriller with all its gorgeous absurdities full blown. . . It is characteristic of the *genre* that the son of a dope-sniffing baronet should be an Honourable. . . . '

When the time came to revise the story for a 1967 paperback edition the (to me) astounding changes in my own style almost made me decide to close the book and forget it. Perhaps I should have done just this. But I confess to a positive *liking* for those 'gorgeous absurdities', and I could not bring myself to remove any of them—nor even to turn my son of a baronet into the son of a peer or else take out his 'Hon'!

John Creasey

# Contents

# 1

# TRAGEDY AT THE CARILON CLUB

Anthony Barr Carruthers sat in the reading-room of the Carilon Club, Pall Mall, London West, and stared morosely at the *Morning Star,* which he held in front of him.

He had been some time locating the single line of information which he wanted, for although familiar with the sporting page, he was a complete stranger to that controlled by the City editor.

His trouble was simple. On the recommendation of a man who should have known better, he had recently purchased ten thousand one-pound shares in Marritaba Tin. Within a week of the deal, his ten thousand had sunk to five, in ten days it had been shaved to two and a half, and now it was somewhere in the region of one thousand seven hundred.

Carruthers glanced again at the damning figures in the City column, then tossed the newspaper to the floor.

His back was towards the door of the Carilon Club's reading-room, and he heard it open, but did not trouble himself to look round. Even had he done so, he would have seen only the sober figure of Rickett, the Carilon Club's secretary, and would not have been conscious of any immediate danger.

Rickett was a typical club secretary, a shadowy individual who was never obvious but always present, rarely speaking, but always having the last word.

As Anthony Barr Carruthers sank back in his armchair and cursed the name of the man who had advised him to buy Marritaba, Rickett moved silently across the room. His suede shoes made no sound on the thick pile carpet, and his breathing was soft and regular. His right hand was in his trouser pocket.

A sudden breeze, coming through the wide-open windows of the reading-room, carried a blast of sultry air into Carruthers's face, and jerked him into irritable motion. He snapped his fingers viciously.

'Damn Riordon!' he muttered aloud. 'I reckon he fleeced me. . . . "

Had he turned at that moment and seen the strange, unquestionably evil smile on Rickett's face, he might have saved himself from the undreamed-of peril. For Rickett was within a yard of him now, moving silently, furtively, towards Carruthers's chair. His right hand was half out of his pocket, and the slanting rays of the sun, coming through the open window, glinted on steel.

As he drew nearer, Rickett stretched out his hand. If Carruthers had thrown his head backwards, he would have felt the sharp prick of a needle in his scalp, and might yet have saved himself. But he kept still, unthinking, unsuspecting.

Then Rickett thrust his hand out, sharply, stabbing the needle of the hypodermic syringe into the fleshy part of Carruthers's neck, pressing his thumb firmly on the lever.

Carruthers gave a sharp cry, and swung round in his chair. In his last moment of consciousness he saw the face of Rickett, twisted in that strange smile.

'What the devil!' gasped Carruthers.

He tried, desperately, to jump to his feet, but his limbs were paralysed—then, with one convulsive shudder, he slumped back in the chair.

Rickett moved quickly over the prostrate body of his victim. He felt Carruthers's pulse, and found only the stillness of death. Without a second glance he turned away and hurried out of the room.

# 2

# HUGH DEVENISH IS
# THOUGHTFUL

'I—I mean,' stammered Aubrey Chester, glancing nervously round the crowded lounge of the Carilon Club, 'this place gives me the creeps, old son. It's like a bally graveyard. If I hadn't promised to meet you here, Hughie, I don't think I could have turned the old toes towards the golden gates. I—I mean...'

He broke off as a waiter bore down on the table at which he sat, together with Hugh Devenish.

'You wouldn't have been able to turn the old toes,' laughed Devenish, 'towards the golden gates. Did you know Carruthers well?' he added more seriously.

Chester shrugged his shoulders.

'Well enough,' he said, 'and yet not so well as I might, Hughie. A nice bird, don't you think? Sport and all that, never said no if you wanted to raise the stakes. The last man in the world,' Chester went on with a puzzled frown, 'you'd have thought anyone'd want to bump off. I can't understand it, really I can't.'

4

The waiter slid away from the table, and as soon as he was out of earshot, Chester leaned forward, peering expectantly into Hugh's eyes.

'I s-say,' he stammered—he always stammered more under the stress of a new idea—'you don't know anything, do you, old scout?'

Hugh Devenish grinned lazily.

'If you mean anything about Carruthers,' he said, 'I don't know a thing. Apart,' he added, 'from what I read in the morning papers.'

'That's where I got it from,' said Chester, with the air of a man who obtains his information straight from the horse's mouth. 'Killed within half a minute, they say, while he was sitting in the reading-room.' Aubrey shivered. 'I don't think I shall ever be able to go in there again, Hughie. Every time I sat down I'd wonder whether I was going to get up again.'

Devenish chuckled, and lit his friend's cigarette.

'You want a nice long sea trip,' he advised, 'to get your nerves back to normal. But joking apart, I had a nasty jar when I read about the murder. I wonder why they picked on Tony?'

Aubrey shrugged his shoulders, suddenly tiring of the subject.

'I don't know,' he allowed. 'B-but you'd better finish your drink, old man. I o-ordered dinner for eight. C-coming?'

The two men strolled across the lounge towards the dining-room, while a dozen or so others nodded a greeting.

Both Devenish and Chester were well-known members of the Carilon, but for some months past Devenish had been abroad. He spent a great deal of time in some unnamed country, wherein he did many things, according to his narrations, which made Aubrey, amongst others, suspect that 'abroad' covered a multitude of activities concerning which Devenish resolutely refused to talk seriously.

Those who knew him well accepted his casual explanation of his numerous disappearances from the social round, and guessed, shrewdly, at the nature of them. Those who knew him slightly dubbed him 'rake' and regretted that they were never invited to sample his amusements.

On the day of Anthony Barr Carruthers's murder, Hugh Devenish had actually been in Paris. The following day he had travelled on the morning train to London, and his first intimation of the murder was the flaring headlines of the overseas *Morning Sun*. On his arrival he had endeavoured to forget the tragedy, and had occupied himself in unpacking his trunks—he had been away for three months, but had luggage enough for three years, according to the unvoiced opinion of Pincher, his man-of-many-duties—and generally settling in at his Clarges Street flat.

A week later he telephoned Aubrey Chester, arranging to meet him at the Carilon Club.

In appearance, they were an ill-matched couple. Chester was a tall, pale, straggly-looking individual, with a small head, thin, sloping shoulders, and a slouch of a walk.

Hugh Devenish, on the other hand, was solidly-built, loose-limbed and broad-shouldered, his skin tanned bronze by a life which rarely kept him indoors for more than a few hours at a stretch, his face rugged rather than handsome.

It had been due to a mutual interest in sport that the two men had, in their early days, first met. But whereas Chester was an excellent tennis-player, Devenish had concentrated almost entirely on cricket.

The friendship, despite Devenish's lengthy absences from London, had lasted well.

They were at the fish course when a short, rotund little man descended upon them like a private tornado and dragged a chair to their table.

Devenish smiled a greeting. 'Marcus, my dear fellow. And how is the modern Croesus standing the strain?'

There was a certain accuracy in his quip; the Hon. Marcus Riordon had a remarkable aptitude for making money.

Riordon chuckled, and stuck a cigarette into a long holder.

'Always busy, Hughie, always showing folk how to make a fortune—don't mind if I smoke, do you?—and how's the traveller? Have a good time?'

'You know Paris,' smiled Devenish.

Riordon smiled back. It was said that he was the best connoisseur of attractive women in London.

Throughout the meal, which he eyed with the envy of one whose appetite is regulated by the outside measurement of his waistband, all three men maintained an irregular flow of conversation.

Rickett, who occasionally unbent from his hauteur to render direct service to his more favoured members, served coffee.

Without appearing to do so, Devenish looked hard at the secretary of the Carilon Club. The murder of Tony Carruthers had created a sensation in London, and the Carilon Club was now the most talked-of place in town. As its secretary, Charles Rickett had been marked down for more publicity than he had ever had in his life. No daily paper had appeared without its short history of 'M'sieu Rickett'—the 'M'sieu' was inspired by the fact that Rickett's parentage was partly French—and the horde of reporters which had engulfed the Club for the past week had been equalled only by the number of detectives, great and small, who had interrogated its staff.

It must, Devenish thought, have been a difficult time for the secretary.

Rickett was a well-built man of medium height. His dark hair was brushed back from his forehead, the set of his shoulders suggesting both physical fitness and strength. Looking at him now, Devenish wondered if he imagined that flicker of fear in the man's eyes—normally so inscrutable.

As the secretary moved away, with a murmured hope that they had found everything to their satisfaction, all three men looked after him.

'There's a man,' commented Riordon, 'who's having a rough time of it, poor devil—don't you think so, Hugh?'

Devenish grinned cheerfully.

'He'll get through it and forget it, Marcus. I shouldn't put Rickett down as a victim of nerves or sentiment.'

Riordon cocked an inquiring eye.

'Why—don't you like him?'

'My poor ass,' drawled Devenish, 'why the blazes should I dislike him? Rickett's the right man for the job; it'd take more than a crowd of flatfoots to put him off his stroke. By the way, Marcus—did you know Carruthers well?'

The question came unexpectedly, and took the Hon. Marcus Riordon off his guard. For a fraction of a second there was a gleam of uncertainty in his eyes, but it disappeared quickly—though Devenish noticed that as he answered he lit a fresh cigarette, without putting it into his holder.

It was part of Devenish's 'business' to notice things. At that particular moment he noticed that the Hon. Marcus Riordon was nervous.

He was interested, chiefly because there appeared to be no reason for nervousness.

'Well,' puffed Riordon, 'I couldn't say I knew him well, if you know what I mean, Hughie—but he told me he'd been losing a lot of money lately—races and whatnot, the idiot—and to tell you the truth I rather wondered at first whether he hadn't killed himself.'

Aubrey Chester swallowed hard and excitedly.

'Th-that's an idea!' he agreed. 'D-do you think th-there's any chance of it, Hugh?'

Devenish lit a cigarette, and waited until the first coil of smoke had wafted upwards before he answered. He appeared to be looking quizzically at his friend, but actually he was observing the bright face of Marcus Riordon.

'I would say there wasn't a chance in a thousand,' he answered at last. 'Tony couldn't have killed himself with a hypodermic syringe without leaving the thing somewhere—'

Riordon picked him up rapidly.

'You can't say that,' he protested. 'Carruthers might have jabbed the thing in his neck and then thrown it out of the window for anyone to come along and pick it up—it isn't impossible.'

Devenish puckered his forehead.

'I hadn't thought of that,' he said. 'Point to you, Marcus. But someone would have to find the thing.'

Chester leaned forward excitedly.

'A k-kid might have picked it up,' he reasoned, 'and n-not think there was anything in it. C-couldn't he, now? Or s-someone who didn't know what it was?'

Devenish shrugged his shoulders.

'The mystery solved,' he said dryly. 'You'd better double along to Scotland Yard while you can remember it all, Marcus. And on the way you can think of a reasonable explanation why Carruthers, *if* he killed himself, stuck the needle in his neck, instead of in his wrist.'

Aubrey Chester gaped as a remarkable thought occurred to him. He stared at Devenish in astonishment.

'I-in his . . .' he began, then winced as Devenish kicked him deliberately on the shin. 'I-in his wrist would have been much easier,' Aubrey improvised hastily, 'b-but you can never t-tell, Hughie. I-I say! I-it's turned h-half past-time! We'll have to b-be shifting—'

Ten minutes later, Devenish and Chester left the golden gates of the Carilon Club and turned right, towards the Admiralty Arch. Devenish said nothing as they walked briskly along. Chester, unusually silent too, wondered why his friend had stopped him from commenting on the fact that Carruthers had been poisoned by an injection in the neck.

They reached Trafalgar Square before Devenish spoke. Then he punched Chester deliberately in the ribs, and grinned tantalisingly.

'Go home and think it out,' he said. 'I've got a date. Thanks for the steak and onions, and come round to me in the morning if you're not playing with that soft ball of yours. Bye.'

It was, Chester said afterwards, much nearer goodbye than either of them dreamed. For a few seconds the tennis player had a dreadful vision of his friend lying stretched out in the road, sent flying by the car which roared suddenly along the Mall and flashed madly beneath the Admiralty Arch.

It was on top of Hugh Devenish as he stepped off the pavement into the road. Only the sudden opening of the car's throttle warned him in time to avoid the fierce rush. With a bigger effort than he had ever made in his life, Devenish leapt desperately for the pavement. The car roared past him. The handle of the door struck him in the small of the back, sending him flying against Aubrey's figure, and the two men went sprawling to the ground!

When they picked themselves up, bruised, dazed and shaken, the car had merged with the cluster of traffic which swung round towards Haymarket, and had disappeared.

# 3

# DEPARTMENT 'Z' AT WHITEHALL

After convincing his friend that the blow in the back had left nothing but a painful bruise, Hugh Devenish waved a cheery hand, and sent Chester homewards, muttering to himself on the iniquity of the owner of this particular car and the need for the death sentence on every driver convicted of passing the thirty mile per hour mark in London. Aubrey, in fact, was annoyed by the incident.

Had he known what was in Hugh's mind, his annoyance would have been drowned in a sea of consternation. Unlike Hugh, he had caught no glimpse of the driver who had so nearly caused a tragedy—he had not, in other words, recognised, or thought he recognised, the heavy features of the ex-prize-fighter who earned a profitable living as the Hon. Marcus Riordon's chauffeur.

Devenish crossed Trafalgar Square warily.

He was not only puzzled; he was perturbed. For unless he was backing the wrong horse, the Hon. Marcus Riordon knew something about Tony Carruthers's death.

Devenish turned into Whitehall, crossed the road to Scotland Yard, and took the first turning to the right beyond it. The narrow street along which he walked was bordered on both sides by towering precipices of bricks and mortar, stone-faced buildings with countless windows and an occasional heavy oak door approached by a flight of grey stone steps.

As he reached one of these doors, Devenish took a quick glance behind him. Satisfied that he was unobserved, he walked quickly up the steps and entered the building, opening the door with a key of a peculiar design. There were only seven such keys in existence.

Walking quietly along the wide passage of the house, from which a dozen doors opened into a dozen apartments set apart for the duties of civil servants working for the Foreign Office, he came to a narrow flight of stairs leading from a recess which a stranger would have passed without a second glance. Climbing these stairs, he reached a small landing, empty of everything but a single oak-faced door. Devenish stopped and pressed his finger on a slight protuberance in the centre of the door.

For a moment he stood quite still, enveloped by the unnatural silence of the deserted building. Then, without a sound, the door slid to the right, disappearing into a hollow in the wall.

A blaze of electric light illuminated the landing in a vivid yellow glare. Devenish narrowed his eyes against it, and stepped forward into the room beyond. The sliding door closed behind him as noiselessly as it had opened.

Then the silence was broken by a thin, dry voice, coming from the humorous mouth of a man who sat at a large mahogany desk, a desk empty of everything beyond a single telephone and a file of papers.

'Hallo, Hugh,' greeted Gordon Craigie. 'Sit down a minute, will you?'

Devenish smiled, and lowered himself into an easy chair drawn up by a cheerful coal fire at the far end of the room.

He had never quite reconciled himself to the office of Gordon Craigie, that man whose name was rarely whispered, even in high circles, but whose reputation was second to none in the diplomatic circles of Whitehall.

The room was split into two parts, divided by an invisible line starting from the sliding—and to the initiated, steel-lined—door.

At the one end was Craigie's desk, which never held more than one file of papers at a time. Two steel cabinets in the wall behind the desk completed the office furnishing.

At the other end of the room were two arm-chairs, drawn up by the fire which burned, day in, day out, winter and summer. A large wooden cupboard, whose door was usually wide open, revealed a clutter of domestic odds and ends. Collars, ties and handkerchiefs rubbed shoulders with a half-full jar of marmalade. A tea-caddy elbowed a half-pound tin of Four Square tobacco.

This office-cum-bed-sitting-room—Craigie often slept in one of the arm-chairs which was of the convertible variety—was all that existed of 'Z' Department at Whitehall.

The ministrations and ramifications of 'Z' Department were innumerable. It was the headquarters of that much-maligned institution, the English Secret Service, and it was said that nothing ever happened of importance in the affairs of any country from Soviet Russia to Timbuctoo which was not eventually reported, coded and filed in Gordon Craigie's office—or his mind.

Craigie was a tall, spare man, with finely cut features set in a much-lined face. He looked like a great hawk, alert, watchful, and full of a latent strength of limb and an obvious strength of mind.

The agents of 'Z' Department loved this man who controlled their destinies. Craigie was a hard taskmaster, sparing in praise, but never condemning failure. The tasks which he set were mountainous, the help he gave in the carrying out of them negligible. If a man worked for 'Z' Department he knew that his chances of getting away with his life in the long run, were small—but when Craigie gave his orders, no one backed out.

On the night of Hugh Devenish's return from Paris on a mission which had been accomplished with some success and a remarkably clean bill of health, Craigie was smoking his pipe—an inevitable meerschaum—as he worked quietly on the file of papers in front of him.

For ten minutes Devenish leaned back in his chair, pulling at an old briar. He heard Craigie push his chair back at last, and looked across the room.

Craigie came over, and the two men shook hands. There was a gleam in the Chief's shrewd eyes, and a smile on his lips, but Devenish, who knew his man well, saw that Craigie was thinking hard about something that did not concern his most successful agent at that moment.

Craigie dropped into the other chair, and pulled his pouch from the capacious pocket of an old smoking jacket.

'I suppose I've got to congratulate you,' he said, stuffing the bowl of his meerschaum with lean, deliberate fingers. 'You'll want a rest, now, I suppose.'

Devenish grinned.

'That means you've another game in the offing,' he hazarded correctly. 'Trot it out while you feel like it.'

Craigie lit his pipe thoughtfully.

'I don't know that I'm ready to talk about it yet,' he said slowly. 'I'll send for you in a day or two, Hugh.' His eyes bored into those of his friend. 'What brought you along?' he asked quietly.

Devenish slid further down in his chair, pursing his lips thoughtfully.

'I don't know,' he acknowledged, 'that it's really a job for us. It's probably more in the flatfoot's line, by the look of it.'

'Well?' interrogated Craigie, who rarely wasted words.

Devenish took the plunge.

'I was at the Carilon tonight,' he said quietly. 'The general topic was poor old Carruthers. Do you know anything about that, Gordon?'

'I know he was poisoned with *adenia,* injected by a hypodermic needle in the neck.'

'You're sure about the neck?'

Craigie nodded.

'Yes. The newspapers called it the wrist, and we—the Yard men, that is—haven't bothered to correct them.'

'Are you sure none of the dailies got hold of the right story?' persisted Devenish.

'Certain of it, Hugh.'

'Hm-hm,' muttered Devenish, wrinkling his forehead. 'I met a man at the Carilon,' he went on, 'who knew that the hole was in Carruthers's neck.'

It was, after all, startling enough information to make even Craigie sit up.

'That's worth knowing,' he commented. 'Who was it, Hugh?'

'That's the funniest part of it. In fact, if I hadn't been nearly run down by his chauffeur half an hour ago, I'd say that it was a slip of the tongue, and that he said "neck" by accident.—'

Craigie whistled.

'Nearly run down, were you?'

'Just beneath the Admiralty Arch,' said Devenish. 'I didn't have much time, but I managed to jump clear. Of course, it might have been an accident, but forty-five miles an hour in that part of the world takes some explaining. And I'd know that chauffeur's face out of a million.'

Craigie took his pipe from his mouth, and tapped it against the fireplace.

'Well,' he inquired at length. 'Who's the bad man, Hugh? Anyone we know?'

Devenish smiled.

'I should say that he's one of the best known men in London, Gordon, and somehow my tongue sticks at naming him. Still—how does the Hon. Marcus Riordon strike you as a potential murderer?'

Devenish finished his words with the air of a man who has thrown a bomb and is waiting for it to burst. But Craigie had prepared himself for the unexpected—or so Devenish thought.

'Riordon, was it?' murmured Craigie.

'Yes, it was the Hon. Marcus. If it had been his begetter, now. . .'

'You'd think his father capable of it, would you?'

Devenish shrugged his shoulders.

'Riordon Senior's a queer cuss,' he pointed out. 'No one really knows much about him, apart from the approximate size of his bank balance, which is large even for the millionaire governors of big banks. But Marcus . . .'

Devenish broke off, more perturbed than he admitted at the possibility of Marcus Riordon's complicity in the attempted murder of him, and in the murder of Tony Carruthers. But his perturbation was lost in astonishment as Craigie, getting quickly from his chair and fetching the file of papers which he had been studying when Devenish had entered the office, opened the file at a page headed '*Carruthers, Anthony Barr,*' and thrust it under his nose.

Devenish read the brief paragraph quickly, his eyes widening as he reached the end.

*Carruthers was murdered* (he read) *in the reading-room of the Carilon Club at or about three-forty-five p.m. on Thursday, twelfth of September. Method—poison injected by needle in nape of neck. Poison used—adenia. Position of body suggests victim was attacked while sitting in chair. Reason for reference to 'Z', newspaper, the Morning Sun, near body was opened at City page, with pencilled mark against quotation for Marritaba Tin Shares. C.I.D. report Carruthers purchased ten thousand one pound shares in Marritaba Tin on twenty-seventh August. Shares valueless. Comments. . . .*

Devenish put the file down, with a terse comment.

'That's the job I had in mind for you,' said the Chief of 'Z' Department, watching his friend closely.

Devenish whistled.

'So it is our meat,' he commented. 'Damn it, Gordon—I knew Tony Carruthers for ten years, and I don't remember that he ever touched anything on the Exchange in his life. Why on earth did the poor devil buy Marritabas?'

'I can ask you a better one than that,' said Craigie. 'Why did he buy Marritabas with his last ten thousand pounds? What had he done with the two hundred thousand pounds that he inherited twelve months ago?'

Devenish scowled.

'So he lost two hundred thousand in a year, did he?'

'And only lived at the rate of five thousand for that year,' complemented Craigie.

'Damn it!' exploded Devenish, roused out of his usual calm, 'Carruthers wasn't that kind of fool. He liked a flutter, but . . .'

Craigie stood up slowly.

'Carruthers *was* that kind of fool,' he said quietly. 'I think you'll find, Hugh, that he gambled, under assumed names, through various brokers, until he lost pretty well a quarter of a million. And I believe, too, that he bought shares on advice that seemed sound. . . Riordon's advice. And I think Riordon killed him, so that he couldn't spread his story around. You'd better have a shot at the job, Hugh. It's part of a bigger one, unless I'm mistaken, but I'm darned if I can find where it's really starting from.'

Devenish frowned.

'Riordon seems pretty near the spot,' he commented.

'Father or son?' demanded Craigie cryptically.

# 4

# SIR BASIL RIORDON, BART.

The wealth of Sir Basil Riordon, Bart., was as well known as his identity was something of a mystery. But for some years he had rarely appeared in public, choosing rather to remain in the background, a legendary, rather frightening figure, a Midas of the Moderns, controlling Bleddon's Bank and its innumerable subsidiaries through his puppet directors and managers.

Bleddon's Bank flourished as it had never flourished before. Financial undertakings which had been large before Sir Basil Riordon had retired into obscurity, now became colossal. Bleddon's financed some of the greatest ventures in the Near and Far East, in Russia, and in South America. Rarely a day passed when the City page failed to announce some fresh venture, and never an appeal for funds failed to receive the support it needed.

Hugh Devenish knew of these things vaguely, as a City clerk hears of the adventures of heroes in the Arctic regions, of dare-devils over Everest. His own fortune, which showed him a comfortable three thousand a year, was as yet untouched by the ramifications of the Riordon companies, and he had never worried himself to keep up to date with the City page.

On the evening of his return from Craigie's office, however, he studied a welter of facts and figures. He wanted a general understanding of the extent of the Riordon financial undertakings.

It was half past two when Devenish finished his reading, and three o'clock when he eventually slid between the sheets, dead tired, but with the tight-chested feeling of the man who knows that he is on the verge of momentous happenings.

How close to the verge even Hugh Devenish did not know.

The Hon. Marcus Riordon picked up the speaking tube in his car, and spoke briskly to the ex-bruiser who was driving along the Haymarket.

That's enough, Huggett,' he said. 'Put me down at Brook Street.'

Ten minutes later, just as Hugh Devenish was entering the office of 'Z' Department, the Hon. Marcus opened the door of his Brook Street flat and walked along the well-carpeted passage, whistling under his breath to conceal a certain mental perturbation.

He knew that he had made a bad gaffe when he had let slip the word 'neck'—and what was worse, he knew that Devenish had noticed it. The estimation which he held for Devenish's capability was demonstrated by the speed with which he had endeavoured to send him out of the land of the living.

The fact that the attempt had failed made Riordon ill tempered. Devenish would be on the *qui vive* for him now, whatever happened. The Hon. Marcus knew that he would have to hasten the completion of the plans which he had been maturing for some years past.

As he turned into his sitting-room, a little surprised that the blue-shaded light was glowing, someone stirred.

Riordon snapped his fingers irritably as he saw the woman who was waiting for him. He had forgotten that Lydia would be there.

As she saw his frown, the woman's face twisted in an unpleasant smile. Lydia Crane knew him too well to keep up a pretence of affection, or even liking.

'You seem pleased,' she drawled sarcastically, as he dropped on to a settee and lit a cigarette. 'Forgotten me again, Marcus?'

'Yes,' he said harshly, 'I had. I wish to heaven I could get rid of you altogether.'

Without his mask of *bonhomie,* Riordon's speech lost its breathless rush. His voice grated at the back of his throat, and his eyes, so often beaming with affected good will to all men, were like pieces of granite.

Lydia Crane laughed mirthlessly.

She was taller than Riordon, full-figured and possessing an exotic fascination which, five years before, the Hon. Marcus had found irresistible. Her black hair coiled luxuriously round her smooth-skinned, oval face. Her beauty was unquestionable; Riordon would have found her an admirable companion but for one thing—her knowledge of his activities. As he stared at her, irritated, he found his pulse quickening, even while she was laughing at him.

He snapped his fingers again.

'Stop that row,' he snapped. 'I'll put my hands round your neck one of these days, damn you.'

Lydia's lips curled.

'You'd never keep them there,' she taunted.

A moment later, she felt an inward rush of fear. There was a gleam in Riordon's eyes which she had never seen before—an animal ferocity which made her forget his rotund figure, his round, red face.

'I've warned you often enough,' he grated. 'You'd better clear out.'

They stared at each other in silence for a full minute. Riordon's eyes dropped first.

'I'm sorry, Lydia,' he muttered. 'Things aren't going as well as they might—I'm worried out of my life.'

After a moment of strained silence, Lydia Crane shrugged her white shoulders—she was dressed in an evening gown of black velvet, daring and effective, the only flash of colour a deep red rose pinned to the moulded bodice.

'All right, Marcus,' she said quietly. 'Only—it wouldn't harm you to be more reasonable.'

Riordon bit back a hot retort.

'That's the girl,' he said lightly. 'I'll be good, my dear!'

'Good enough to come out?' queried Lydia. 'I've been waiting for hours, and I'm bored to tears.'

Riordon patted her shoulder.

'Yes, we'll go out,' he promised. 'You can ring for a table at the Golden Dawn, while I'm phoning my father. I won't be long.'

He went into his study, the only room in the luxuriously appointed flat which was always kept locked, lifted a telephone from a niche in a large, plain oak desk in one corner of the room, and dialled a number.

A man's ill-tutored voice answered him promptly.

Riordon spoke quietly into the mouthpiece. The gist of his instructions was simple.

'Get Devenish,' he instructed, 'and get him quickly.'

Five minutes later, Riordon called Wharncliff 39. A woman answered him.

'Is that Mr. Marcus?'

'Yes,' said Riordon irritably.

After a brief wait, the woman's voice came again.

'I'm sorry, Mr. Marcus,' she said quietly, 'but Sir Basil is not available. Shall I ask him to ring you back?'

'I'll ring later,' said Riordon, replacing the receiver sharply.

As he went out of the study, locking the door behind him, there was a cruel twist to his lips, a gleam of evil humour in his eyes.

# 5

# DEVENISH GETS A SHOCK

On the morning following his intensive studies of Sir Basil Riordon's activities, Hugh Devenish breakfasted at nine-fifteen. He glanced through the *Morning Star,* and learned that the police expected to make an arrest at any moment in the Carruthers Case.

Half an hour later, he was slipping in the clutch of his Aston Martin, and sliding out of Clarges Street into Piccadilly. Several passers-by looked with undisguised interest at the bronzed face and ruffled fair hair of the man at the wheel. Had they been told that he carried a loaded automatic in his trouser pocket, a second gun of minute proportions strapped to the calf of his left leg, and a thin-bladed knife, a curved electric torch and a number of long waxed matches tied to his right calf, they would have been incredulous, but the particulars would have been true. In addition to this armoury, Devenish carried a thin length of rope twisted around his waist, and a delicate but effective glass-cutter in his breast pocket. A small but powerful camera rested on the seat next to him.

He was aiming for the village of Wharncliff, which nestled between Horsham and Cuckfield in the county of Sussex, and he planned to take a preparatory survey of Wharncliff Hall.

The Hall, a century-old mansion set in the midst of a thick belt of woodland two miles from the main road, had been purchased, three years before, together with two hundred odd acres of downland, by Sir Basil Riordon. It was there that the financial magnate now lived, cutting himself off from all public contact.

At half past eleven Devenish stopped outside a garage.

'How far are we from Wharncliff?'

The proprietor rasped his thumb across his chin.

'Two miles, mebbe, mebbe three.'

'Straight along the road?'

'As straight as you can go,' nodded the man affably. 'Turn right by the Bull, and left at the fork a couple of hundred yards further on. You can't go wrong . . . '

Devenish grinned at this definition of a straight run, opened the door of the car and stepped out. The garage man widened his eyes.

'I'm walking,' Devenish told him genially. 'Look after her for me, will you?'

He slipped a ten-shilling note into the man's willing fingers, and turned towards Wharncliff.

A quarter of an hour's steady walking took him to the Bull. As he pushed open the bar door, the landlord welcomed him with a cheerful smile.

'A fine morning, sir.'

'A thirsty one,' said Devenish, noticing the other two occupants of the saloon, a prosperous-looking farmer, and an old man with a beard. 'Do you sell brown ale?' he added blandly.

The innkeeper laughed.

'In quarts, sir, or gallons?'

'Tankards,' said Devenish, with emphasis. 'Four in number, if you'll join me.'

He waved his hand comprehensively, and the company murmured their appreciation. With the speed obtained through long and accurate practice the landlord planted four tankards of foaming ale on the bar. The farmer and the old man moved from their seat by the window, and the four drank deeply.

'A nice day,' commented Devenish, after a pause.

'Wonderful, for the time of the year,' agreed the farmer jovially. 'I was only saying to Will'um, here. . .'

Devenish, who could take his drink with any man, was in no hurry. He knew the difficulty of turning rustic conversation into the desired channel, and experience had taught him that it turned best if it turned on its own accord.

The farmer eventually inserted the thin edge of the wedge, with his inevitable sigh of regret.

'Aye,' he nodded portentously, 'things aren't what they were, sir, and they're not likely to be, when moneyed folk hold tight to their holdings like they are doing. Prosperity depends on the money that's spent. That's my belief, and it always will be. Another, sir?'

'It's my turn,' said Devenish, untruthfully.

His error was allowed to go uncorrected.

'As I was saying to Will'um,' went on the discursive farmer, eyeing his second tankard of ale thoughtfully, 'it's us poor fools who've got nothing that spend everything. Such as have got it. . .'

'Like the squire,' inserted the old man, with a rueful shake of his beard.

''Tis ruination for the district, the way he's going on,' the landlord put in sadly. 'Why, a year ago there were twenty families living on the estate. . .'

'And now,' complemented the farmer, pessimistically inclined after his second tankard, 'there can't be half a dozen cottages occupied, outside the village . . . '

'One after another,' said the old man, taking up the story as the farmer dipped his nose into his ale, 'they've been given notice to quit. Ah me, sir, 'twere a sad day when the new squire came.'

The arrival of Sir Basil Riordon was not, obviously, a thing about which the locals were glad. He had, Devenish gathered, gradually emptied the cottages on the big Wharncliff estate, until the Hall itself was standing in the middle of the grounds in lonely grandeur.

Why was Riordon deliberately making his home inaccessible? thought Devenish. Why was he deliberately forcing the cottagers out of his land?

Although he posed the question to himself, he realised that the answer was a long way off, but his discoveries added considerably to his interest in Riordon; when he made his report, Craigie would be able to add several pages to his file on the mystery of the banker's activities.

Devenish's companions fell into a brooding silence. There was little more, Devenish thought, that he could learn from them, and with a genial smile he prepared to take his leave. But as he opened his mouth to say goodbye, the words froze on his lips.

From somewhere outside the Bull, shattering the pensive stillness of the bar, came a sudden cry.

*The high, shrill cry of a frightened woman.*

The three countrymen in the saloon bar seemed frozen into immobility. They stared towards the door, as though expecting it to open and admit the Devil himself, their eyes wide open, their lips parted.

They saw Devenish move, like men in a dream.

For a split second after that single cry, Devenish had stood like a man petrified. Then, one hand in his pocket, he leapt towards the door and flung it open.

Outside, a scene which might have come from the high spot of a thriller film met his eyes. Twenty yards from the door of the Bull stood a long black car. A man sat in the driving seat, his hands on the wheel—the engine of the car was humming, the chassis quivering.

On the dusty road, two men and a girl were struggling in a tangled whirlwind of twisting bodies and billowing clouds of dust. Devenish could see the girl's face, white and tense as she fought against her assailants, and even in that hectic moment he saw that she was more than pretty. The two men he summed up in one quick glance. They were toughs of the toughest variety, big, powerful ruffians who could have overpowered their victim in a split second—if they had wanted to.

He was ten yards from the bonnet of the car when the driver saw him. Devenish saw his right hand disappear from the wheel.

Devenish fired from his pocket, on the instant. There was a sound of splintering glass, a sudden, agonised shout, and the driver dropped backwards in his seat, his hands clutching his shoulder.

Devenish hurtled across the intervening space as the two remaining roughnecks dropped the girl and swung round towards the new threat. Both men darted their hands spasmodically towards their pockets. The moment which they lost in going for their guns gave him all the time that he needed.

With every ounce of strength in his body, Devenish struck the first man's chin. For a split second the man's body seemed to leave the ground, then he sagged down with a thud.

The second man tugged desperately at his gun, and the weapon glinted for a moment in the sunlight; but before he could use it, Devenish hit him also. A short cry started from the man's lips, then he too dropped to the ground.

Devenish, breathing hard, looked down at them.

Then he looked across at the girl, who was leaning against the car. The sleeve of her coat was ripped open from shoulder to wrist, and Devenish saw an ugly red bruise on the white flesh of her arm.

He stepped to her side quickly, with a reassuring smile.

'Take it easy,' he advised her. 'No—don't try to talk for a minute, young woman, it'll keep.'

As he spoke, he slipped one arm round her shoulders and the other beneath her knees, and lifted her bodily away from the car. He carried her easily towards the Bull, grinning cheerfully at the stupefied faces of his erstwhile drinking companions, and deposited her on a bench beneath the saloon window.

'That's better,' he said cheerfully. 'Now all you want is a spot of—that's the fellow!' he broke off as the landlord appeared by his side with a tumbler of neat whisky. 'Open wide,' he commanded.

But Devenish did little more than touch the girl's lips. She shook her head and spluttered as the fiery spirit burned her tongue, pulled a wry face, and struggled into a sitting position.

'I'm—all right,' she gasped. 'Take that stuff away, for heaven's sake . . . '

The colour was gradually returning to her cheeks and lips, and she was breathing more steadily. Devenish saw a pair of grey eyes, a short, straight nose above a firm but well-shaped mouth, and a determined chin.

A moment later, the smile which was curving the corners of her lips disappeared. As he stared at the girl he saw her freeze with sudden, inexplicable fear.

She was looking past him, towards something along the road.

Devenish swung round, hand at hip, ready for any emergency, but all he saw was a rather portly old man, muffled up to his chin in spite of the heat of the sun, walking towards them. The man walked with a decided limp, but it was his parchment-like face and his hard, compelling eyes that Devenish stared at with such amazement.

The three men by the door of the inn seemed to stiffen as the old man limped towards them, and Devenish only just caught the whispered words of the landlord.

'Sir Basil himself,' he muttered, turning his head away awkwardly.

The name seemed to dance a fandango in Devenish's brain, but deeper than his surprise was his realisation that the girl was watching the wizened old financier with eyes filled with despairing fear.

# 6

# AND ASSUMES A RESPONSIBILITY

Sir Basil Riordon looked as though he had been living in close confinement, away from the light of day, for years on end. The pallor of his face had a grey, unhealthy tinge.

When he spoke, his voice was cracked and hoarse, like that of a man who has almost forgotten how to use his tongue. There was something unclean, something forbidding, about the gaunt old man.

'I thought,' said Riordon, harshly, speaking directly to the girl and ignoring the existence of Devenish and the others, 'that I had asked you not to leave the Hall today, Miss Dare. May I ask why you did?'

Devenish looked away from the speaker to the girl. The look of fear had disappeared from her eyes, which now seemed clouded, expressionless. Her whole body seemed to droop.

'I'm sorry . . .' she began.

Before she went further, Devenish sneezed. It was a good sneeze, if not a genuine one, and it startled the girl for a moment, making her break off and glance towards him.

Devenish stepped into the breach, his eyes smiling good-humouredly.

'I hope I haven't put my foot in it,' he said to Riordon. 'I had the deuce of a job persuading Miss Dare to come out, but. . .'

Riordon interrupted him coldly.

'I was not aware,' he said icily, 'that I asked for your comments. Miss Dare . . .'

'As I was saying,' persisted Devenish, with no alteration in the smile on his lips, but with a sudden glint in his eyes, 'I was forced to exert what little authority I had over Miss Dare, and she came out entirely against her will. May I have the pleasure of knowing your name?' he added, with a sarcasm which was lost on the trio crowding in the doorway of the Bull.

Whether or not it was lost on Riordon, Devenish could not be sure. He was satisfied that the man turned his eyes towards him for the first time.

'My name is Riordon,' he said harshly. 'Sir Basil Riordon. . ..'

'In which case,' said Devenish, with an apologetic smile, 'I owe you an apology for having persuaded Miss Dare to act against your wishes.'

Riordon's eyes glittered arrogantly.

'That is a matter,' he said, 'which I can discuss with Miss Dare later in the day.'

'Unfortunately,' said Devenish, 'I doubt whether you will have the opportunity. Your. . .' he took a chance—'secretary has to run up to Town on urgent private business.'

Riordon's eyes narrowed.

'I was not aware,' he grated, 'that Miss Dare had any business of a private nature important enough for her to absent herself without my permission.'

Devenish smiled.

'There are a lot of things,' he said easily, 'of which you are not aware, Sir Basil. I can only ask you to take it as definite that Miss Dare is coming to Town with me, and in the event of her non-return to Wharncliff I suggest that you communicate with me . . . '

As he finished, Devenish pulled his wallet from his coat, flipped it open, and with a neat movement handed a slip of pasteboard to the financier.

The card contained a simple statement of his name, and registered the fact that his postal address was 77a Clarges Street, W.l. It was not, normally, a devastating piece of information, but as Riordon read it, his eyes blazed with a sudden fury.

'Devenish!' he spat, glaring at the other's face.

Devenish bowed with mock courtesy.

'At your service. And now, Sir Basil, may I suggest that you discuss the situation with your—er—friends on the pavement, and . . .'

He left the sentence in mid-air and turned to the girl who had risen from the bench and was looking at him with eyes which revealed a deep gratitude, but in which still lurked a shadow of fear. For a moment she seemed to hesitate; then she turned to her employer.

'I am afraid I shall have to go with Mr.—Devenish,' she said, pleasantly but firmly. 'I will write to you, Sir Basil.'

If Riordon heard her, he gave no sign of it. He was still staring at Devenish, who took Miss Dare's elbow, and turned away from the old man's scrutiny, as though forgetting his presence.

The man with the wounded shoulder had got out of the car—a Chrysler—and was standing by one of the roughnecks who had now recovered from his brief contact with Devenish's fist. The second bruiser lay sprawling in the dust, one arm bent under him, his head lolling unpleasantly on one side.

With the girl beside him, Devenish reached the Chrysler and stopped in front of the driver, who twisted his face in an evil grimace.

'I'll get you for this,' he muttered.

'Get moving,' said Devenish, with an edge to his voice.

The man slouched reluctantly away from the car, still muttering threats under his breath.

'Now,' said Devenish to Miss Dare, 'we can be on our way.'

He opened the front passenger-seat door, and before she realised what was happening the girl was being helped into the car. Then Devenish hurried round to the other side, slid into the driving seat, and pressed the starter. The engine whirred, and Devenish slid the car towards the little group of men, clustering round the open doors of the Bull.

Sir Basil Riordon was standing dead still, staring at him with eyes filled with cold hatred. But Devenish reckoned that he could get away with the manoeuvre without any trouble— and he succeeded. Handling the car with easy mastery, he swung it round in the wide patch of road outside the pub, slid perilously close to the glowering toughs, waved them an airy adieu, and let the engine do its best. It had taken him twenty minutes to walk from the garage to the Bull; the return journey took him three.

After settling the girl in the Aston Martin, he conferred for a moment with the garage proprietor, who listened carefully, rubbed his hand against the seat of his trousers and split his lips into a wide grin of understanding. A pound note changed hands, and Devenish got into his car.

The garage proprietor watched the Aston Martin disappear from sight round a bend in the road, looked quickly in the other direction, saw that he was unobserved, and picked a small axe from a medley of tools, lying about the floor of his shed.

With two heavy swings, he pierced the petrol tank of the Chrysler with the axe, and jumped away quickly to avoid the petrol which spurted out with a hiss. Then he dropped the axe, shrugged his shoulders, and prepared to wait until the owners of the damaged car arrived.

It was, he opined, easy money. And if he was any judge, the man with the Aston Martin was fully justified in his animosity towards the three men who had passed the garage in the Chrysler a short while before.

'And so,' said Devenish, explaining his manœuvre with the roughnecks' car to Miss Marion—he learned later—Dare, 'if your little friends feel like following us, they're right in the cart. There isn't another garage for two or three miles, and I doubt whether they'd be able to hire a car there anyway. So we're safe for the next couple of hours.'

He grinned sideways at her.

'And now,' he went on, 'I suppose I've got to apologise for rushing you away like this.'

'Apologise! Good Lord, there's no need to apologise,' she exclaimed. 'I—I really don't know how to thank you for the way you handled Sir Basil.'

Devenish grimaced at the mention of the financier, and pressed his foot down on the accelerator. The wind swept into their faces as the speedometer crept towards the sixty mark, and the countryside flashed by.

'That,' said Devenish, 'was nothing. And now. . .' he paused for a moment—'might we have a sketch of events before you sent out the S.O.S., and I tumbled to it that something was wrong?'

Marion Dare nodded.

'It's difficult,' she said slowly, 'but perhaps I should start by saying that I've worked for Sir Basil for nearly three years, and. . .' she laughed a little ruefully, 'there hasn't been much spare time. When I discovered that he would be away for the morning, I couldn't resist the temptation to come out for a walk.'

She broke off for a moment, as Devenish negotiated a farm cart, and she noticed that he gave the horse and driver plenty of warning and ample room.

'We were saying?' he prompted.

'I reached the main road,' Marion Dare went on, 'just as the Chrysler drew up near the Bull. All three men knew me—they are servants at the Hall—and when the car stopped, one of them came along the road towards me. . .'

'You were walking towards the Bull?' queried Devenish, who wanted the narration as vivid as he could get it.

'Yes,' agreed the girl. 'There's a footpath leading from the road to Wharncliff Hall, which comes out about fifty yards this side of the inn. I wanted a drink—it was hot for walking, and it's nearly two miles to the Hall—and the car was drawn up between me and the Bull. I was within a couple of feet of the man—his name is Rogers, the man you hit first—when Tomlinson, the driver, called out, "he's coming." I didn't know what they meant,' Marion went on quietly, 'but I guessed that they meant someone inside the Bull, and when I looked, I could just see you through the window, turning towards the door . . .'

She broke off for a moment, looking at Devenish, sensing his body stiffen.

'Well,' she said, with an effort, 'I thought at first that they knew you, and you knew them. But I happened to glance down at Huggett's hand—Huggett was your second victim,' she explained, 'and I saw that he was holding a gun.

He didn't mean me to see it, of course, but before I could stop myself, I had cried out. And then, somehow, I seemed to be in the middle of them, and I hardly knew what was happening, when you came flying out of the Bull.'

Devenish knew now that he had been within a few seconds almost of perdition. If Fate had not inspired Marion Dare to take a walk in defiance of her employer's instructions, it would have been a hundred to one on his falling into the ambush laid by Riordon's hirelings. The thought was not a pleasant one.

'My dear,' he said quietly, taking his left hand from the wheel and touching her arm, 'it will take a long time for me to thank you for that.'

Marion Dare looked up at him.

'You've thanked me enough already,' she said. 'I've wanted to break away from Sir Basil for a long time, but—well, it isn't always easy to get a job, and I just couldn't pluck up courage to give him my notice. Now. . .' she forced herself to smile—'I can't very well go back to the Hall.'

'Not by a long chalk, you can't,' Devenish said grimly. 'So you've worked for him during the last three years, have you?'

'Ever since he retired.'

'And a very interesting period,' murmured Devenish, half to himself, 'but that's by the way. Tell me—do you know his son at all?'

He looked down at her as he spoke, and before the words were out of his mouth he saw the shadow race back into her eyes. Her body stiffened, her voice grew bitter.

'You mean Marcus,' she said. 'Yes, I know him as well as I know his father. I think Marcus must be the cruellest man I've ever known!'

# 7

# Marion Dare Makes an Admission

He should have been prepared, Devenish told himself. Sidelights on the younger Riordon's latent instincts for crime had been all too revealing during the past twenty-four hours.

As it was, so taken aback was he that he kept his eyes off the road for at least thirty seconds, and failed to notice the car which swung suddenly round the bend towards him. The Aston Martin was well up on the crown of the road, and for a petrifying moment a smash seemed inevitable. Marion Dare's eyes widened, and she clutched the side of the car tightly.

Devenish gritted his teeth as he swung the wheel round, heading towards the bank. At the crucial moment he slewed it back again. The nearside front wing struck against the bank of the road, the car shuddered under the slight impact, then scraped along the hedge with a cracking of broken twigs.

The margin had been perilously small. As the Aston Martin steadied, the oncoming car roared past it. It was a Bentley S3, a magnificent cream-coloured monster, gleaming beneath the sun, its driver hunched low over the wheel, taking no notice of the car which had so nearly caused a smash.

Devenish had one glance at the driver—and then for the second time that morning, went cold with astonishment.

Why, he demanded of himself a dozen times as he drove Londonwards more carefully, was Lord Aubrey Chester now in the neighbourhood of Wharncliff?

He was still wondering as he pulled up outside his Clarges Street flat and ushered his companion inside. But now he forced it to the back of his mind.

'This,' said Hugh Devenish, grinning broadly at his valet, 'is Miss Marion Dare, Pincher. A very good friend of ours, I can tell you.'

Pincher bowed, slightly and distantly.

He saw that Miss Dare not only wore a coat which was ripped from shoulder to wrist, but that she had an ugly bruise on her forearm and, just above it, a deep scratch.

'If I may say so, sir,' said Pincher, 'it will be wise to treat the—er—wound in Miss Dare's arm. Shall I bring the first aid box?'

Marion shook her head.

'No, please!' she said. 'I'm all right . . . '

But Pincher disappeared into the internal regions, and to the ears of the couple in the living-room of Devenish's flat, there came the faint sounds of activity beyond.

Devenish pulled a chair round for the girl, who sat down gratefully. The wound in her arm was throbbing painfully, and her head ached.

Devenish stood a couple of yards away from her, looking anxiously down at her tousled hair and pale face. Between the lines of her brief self-history he had been able to read the tribulations of her life as the private secretary to Sir Basil Riordon, and he guessed, too, that she would not have been so dubious about leaving her job unless she had been comparatively friendless.

'Pincher's coming,' he said, after a few minutes of silence. 'We'd better have that coat off, Miss Dare. No, don't get up . . .'

He helped her off with the torn jacket.

Pincher, returning from the bathroom, deposited a first aid box on a small table, handing his master a towel and a sponge, and went out of the room again to fetch a bowl of water.

Within ten minutes of the commencement of operations, Marion Dare's souvenir of the struggle on the road was concealed by a neatly fastened bandage. Pincher, moreover, revealed both his versatility and his acceptance of Marion by finding a needle and cotton and running a seam along the torn sleeve.

'It is not,' he said apologetically, 'a first class job, madam, but it will enable you to put the coat on.'

Then he turned to Devenish.

'I was wondering,' he continued, 'whether you will want a cold lunch, sir, or whether, in view of madam's unexpected call, it would be better for me to cook. I can easily grill two steaks, and if you will allow me to presume so far, I would suggest that I. . .'

'I'll give you half an hour,' said Devenish, 'and not half a minute more.'

Pincher expressed his triumph by a slight flicker of his heavily-lidded eyes, bowed slightly towards the guest, still more slightly towards his master, then turned out of the room.

Devenish looked at his guest.

'I suppose,' he said, quietly, 'that you don't know why the gentlemen on the road handled you so roughly and yet not so roughly as they might, do you?'

Marion gave a bitter little laugh.

'I can guess,' she said. 'They thought that Sir Basil, or his son, might hear that they'd—manhandled—me, and they didn't know how the Riordons would take it.'

Devenish worried the stem of his pipe with his teeth.

'Living in fear,' he suggested.

'I suppose you could call it that,' agreed Marion. 'Several times the men have been caught doing something that the Riordons didn't like, and—well,' she ended, with a shrug, 'they've just disappeared.'

'Do you say "disappeared" intentionally, or do you mean that they were fired?'

'I don't know. One day they would be about the house and the next they would be missing. No one seemed to know where they'd gone . . .'

'Who do you mean by "no one"?' prompted Hugh.

'None of the other servants,' answered Marion. 'I knew all of them fairly well, of course, and we used to chat occasionally. But—well, it's hard to explain.'

Devenish waved his hands in mock surprise.

'What about all that female chatter we hear so much about?' he teased.

Marion's answer made him raise his brows.

'The only woman permanently at the Hall, besides myself,' she said, evenly, 'was Mrs. Ransome, the house-keeper. All the rest were men. Sometimes Marcus brought a woman down with him for a day or two, but there was only one who came down more than once. She—her name is

Lydia Crane—came down fairly often, actually—the others came in between.'

Devenish laughed.

'So Marcus has a real attachment,' he commented. 'That might be worth knowing. And now there's just one more question I want to ask—but I'd like you to know that it's not just for the sake of curiosity. It's this. When you saw Sir Basil, you looked frightened. I won't say you *were,* but you looked it. . .'

Marion Dare interrupted him.

'I was,' she admitted tensely.

'And yet,' Devenish went on, 'you told me you were anxious to get away from the Hall. And,' he added, gently, 'good jobs aren't all *that* difficult to get.'

Marion Dare spoke quietly.

'I've been afraid of the Riordons, father and son, almost from the time I worked for them,' she said. 'All of us who worked there were the same, I think,' she added, with a slightly higher tone. 'We hated them.'

'Why?'

Marion shrugged her shoulders in a helpless gesture.

'I just don't know,' she said. 'It wasn't anything they did or said—at least, not at first. But Sir Basil always seemed to be watching, wherever I went. If I went into the grounds, he nearly always sent someone after me, and even when I moved about the house, he seemed to know where I was going. It was like—like being in prison!'

'I hope,' said Devenish, with a mock severity, 'that you haven't had any first hand experience of prison walls, my dear Miss Dare . . .'

And then he stopped.

For Marion Dare's expression changed from one of trouble and fear to one of agony, that agony of the mind which is a thousand times harder to bear than agony of the body. She leaned forward in her chair, staring at Devenish with hopeless eyes.

'But I have!' she burst out, clenching her fists so that the knuckles gleamed white beneath the stretched skin. 'I have! That's why I was frightened of Riordon—why we all hated him. We were all—jailbirds!'

# 8

# More Trouble with Marritabas

It took Devenish ten minutes to quieten Marion Dare's outburst of dry, body-racking sobbing. At last she squared her shoulders, almost defensively.

'It was nearly four years ago,' she said in a low voice, 'I was working for the Marritaband Development Company—there was a boom in tin shares about that time, if you can remember. . .'

Devenish widened his eyes.

'Tin shares, was it?' he demanded.

Marion hardly noticed his surprise, in her own heavy-heartedness. She went on:

'Yes—the Marritaband Company in England was really the selling organisation of the South American mines. Well—someone stole nearly two hundred pounds from the safe. Only three of us knew the combination of it, and the other two, besides myself, were the directors. There—there was only one conclusion that they could come to, of course.

They prosecuted, and I had a—year's sentence...' Marion broke off, tears blinding her eyes.

'I see,' said Devenish, his voice suddenly gentle. 'It was a kind of frame-up, and you were the picture.'

Marion Dare looked up at him.

'I sometimes wonder,' she said, bitterly, 'whether I did actually take the money or not. It was found in my room, mostly, and some of the notes were traced in the shops that I had visited. And when I told the—police—that I hadn't touched the safe, they took no notice. No one believed me. Even when I came out of—prison—no one who heard that I had been—inside—believed that I was innocent.'

Devenish wanted to talk, to tell her he understood, but somehow he couldn't form the words. He waited for her to speak again.

After a while she went on dully, 'I gave up trying to get work through the ordinary channels, and registered with an association which looks after people like—myself. I think they called it Discharged Prisoners Welfare Association. Eventually Sir Basil Riordon offered me a job at his country house. He sent Marcus—and Marcus was blunt about it. His father wanted someone to work, not to play, and if I had any scruples about taking the job, would I turn it down without hesitation? Well. . .' she broke off, 'you know the rest pretty well.'

Devenish nodded thoughtfully.

'Except,' he said, 'the reason why you think Marcus is—cruel, didn't you call it?'

Marion closed her eyes, wearily. Devenish knew that she was very near to breaking point, and he determined that after her answer, the subject would be dropped completely.

'Well,' she said slowly. 'I didn't like Sir Basil. I *hated* him. But he was an old man, and his son meant a great deal to him. He used to count the hours when Marcus was coming to see him. But practically every time he came, Marcus had a terrible quarrel with his father—and afterwards, Sir Basil would be ill for a week, or even longer.'

'Ill?' queried Devenish.

'He kept to his bed,' said Marion, 'and a doctor—a Frenchman who came to the Hall regularly every week— was with him all the time. I could hear him shouting, even screaming, sometimes.'

'My God!' thought Devenish. But there was no need to upset the girl.

'I see,' he said quietly. 'It was a nasty break, Marion. But I think we can forget it now.'

It was two o'clock when lunch was finished, and Devenish lit a cigarette, discovering that Marion preferred not to smoke.

Then, after a consultation with Pincher, he presented the girl with an array of cushions, and told her that she needed a rest.

Marion agreed, gratefully, and Devenish led her to the spare bedroom of the flat.

When he returned, Pincher was standing respectfully by the dining-room table, which was still littered with the remains of the meal. It looked, Devenish said, as though he was expecting something.

'I was just waiting,' said Pincher chidingly, 'for any instructions, sir.'

'You're a liar,' said Devenish, smiting his valet heavily on the back, without causing the minutest change in expression. 'You were waiting for information, Pincher, inspired by your incurable curiosity.'

'As you wish,' bowed Pincher.

Devenish frowned.

'Pincher,' he said, without further preamble, 'there's a lot of heavy weather in the offing.'

'I assumed that there was, sir,' murmured Pincher.

'And,' continued Devenish, 'I've got a hell of a lot to do, and it can't all be done here. At the same time, and with all respect to you, I don't feel easy about leaving you alone with Miss Dare. It is just possible that others might be curious as to our guest's present quarters. Now —haven't you got a sister, Pincher?'

'I have, sir.'

'With a tough husband?'

'Wiggings,' said Pincher, with a disparaging wave of the hand, 'was a prize-fighter, as you know, Mr. Devenish.'

'And they live a life of laziness and luxury in Chelsea, don't they?'

'They live in Chelsea,' concurred Pincher, evenly.

'I was wondering,' murmured Devenish, 'whether you feel you could put up with the tough husband's company— and your sister's, of course—for a day or two. If you telephoned them, and asked them to come over right away, do you think they could fix it? Then,' he explained, 'I could leave you, confident that any callers who refused to be dismissed by your—er—tact, could be biffed when and as necessary by Wiggings.'

Pincher's brows went upwards, towards his dome-like forehead.

'Without wishing to be at all disrespectful,' he said smoothly, 'I may say, Mr. Devenish, that I suspected the possibility of events developing in this manner, and took the liberty of communicating by telephone with my sister, who assures me that it will be quite convenient for her and

Wiggings to visit here. I have only to call them again, sir, and they will come at once.'

Resplendent in an exquisitely-cut Savile Row suit, Hugh Devenish stepped quietly to the door of the spare room, and after a preliminary, almost inaudible tap, opened the door silently, and poked his head into the room.

Marion Dare was lying full length on the bed. Devenish drew in a deep breath as he saw her, for the first time, peacefully asleep, and with the worry and fear missing from her features.

He stood for a moment, looking down at her, then drew away, and closed the door silently behind him.

Five minutes later, he walked briskly down the steps, leading from 77a into Clarges Street, looked quickly to right and left but without appearing to glance in either direction, and stepped into the driving seat of the Aston Martin. The engine turned quietly into motion, and Devenish slipped in the clutch.

Before touching any speed, he dipped his hand into his waistcoat pocket for his cigarette case—he rarely smoked his pipe out-of-doors—and let the case slip out of his fingers.

For the second time that day, Fate smiled on him.

As he bent down to retrieve the case, something smacked into the windscreen, drilled a small, round hole through the safety glass, and hummed over his head.

Devenish tightened his lips as he heard the low-pitch easily recognisable hum. His body went tight, and he kept well down, screwing his head round and looking at the hole in the glass. As he saw it, a second bullet smacked through, then a third, and a fourth.

Someone was firing, Devenish knew, from a house on the right hand side of the road, and was firing either from a window, or from the top of the steps leading up to the front door.

For the moment, he did not concern himself with the murderous nature of the attack. Somehow he had to get out of the second ambush that had been made for him that day.

After the fourth shot, the bullets stopped, but Devenish knew that as soon as he poked his head up above the dashboard, they would start again.

Crouching beneath the safety line, his mind worked at lightning speed. He knew that Clarges Street, at that hour of the day, was likely to be deserted for five or even ten minutes on end. There were no tradesmen on their rounds, the afternoon exodus of nursemaids had not started, and only the casual wayfarer was likely to turn into the street.

The seconds passed like minutes. He had one great fear—that the attacker was, in fact, inside one of the houses, and that he would be shooting next from a top floor window. The dashboard would afford him no protection if the shooting started from a higher angle.

He forced himself to be cautious, however, and without lifting his head or shoulders, managed to raise one hand sufficiently to press the self-starter, while with the other he slammed the car into gear. The engine whirred, and as he released the hand brake, the car slid forward.

He was driving blind, his head and shoulders still bent low—praying he could keep the car on the road and that he would run into no child or animal. Only a few yards were needed to get him out of the gunman's range.

Suddenly, out of the tail of his eye, he saw a dark ball flying over his head, followed by an ominous wisp of smoke. It was, Devenish realised in an instant of near panic, a bomb—and he knew, with a horrible sinking in the pit of his stomach, that if it landed in the back of the car, it was a thousand to one against him escaping with his life.

His heart in his mouth, Devenish pressed his foot on the accelerator, one hand gripping the wheel above his head, the other fumbling blindly for the horn. The car leapt forward, making him lose his grip, and he grabbed at the wheel desperately, knowing what was coming, thankful for a moment's respite as he heard the bomb drop in the road behind him.

The car twisted towards the kerb. Above the dashboard, Devenish saw a lamp standard looming up in front of him. Swearing beneath his breath, he wrenched the wheel round, and the standard dropped away to his left. The car lurched sickeningly.

Then it happened!

With a devastating roar, the bomb burst. Devenish saw nothing of the vivid red and yellow flash, but felt the car lift bodily upwards from the back, its rear wheels leaving the road a good twelve inches, swaying and rocking from side to side. A rain of shrapnel showered above his head, dropping about him, on his arms, his hands, his shoulders. Several sharp points pierced the backs of his hands.

The car thudded down again, shuddered from bonnet to tail lamp, slithered forward, then jerked to a stop.

Devenish felt a tremendous load lift from his mind. Neither of the rear tyres had been pierced by the flying pieces of steel, and he was within a second or two of safety.

The deafening din of the explosion had hardly settled before a dozen windows opened, and a dozen startled faces peered into the road. From one end of the street—behind Devenish—a policeman came running, the shrill blasts of his whistle echoing between the tall buildings. Two pedestrians turned into the street, running in the policeman's wake, and from a window just above Devenish a woman's voice shrieked out, vibrant, high-pitched.

'There he is—in that porch! In there . . .!'

Devenish forced himself to keep below the dashboard. If he looked over the side of the car, he knew that there was still a possibility of the sharpshooter aiming for him. He heard the thudding of footsteps, the raucous voice of the policeman, the shrieking of the woman. In his mind's eye he could picture his assailant, rushing from the cover of the porch from which he had thrown the bomb, and men who were chasing him. What he did not see—until it was past him—was the low-built car which swung suddenly into Clarges Street from the direction of Piccadilly.

The driver was a uniformed chauffeur, whose heavy features were twisted in a vicious snarl as he swerved into the little crowd of men who were running after the fugitive. The policeman held his arms wide in a plucky effort to send the car on to the pavement, but it only slowed down for a fraction of a second.

In that moment, Devenish's attacker leapt for the rear door, swung it open, and threw himself into the back seat.

Then the driver trod on his accelerator, hunching himself over the wheel as he sent the car swooping onwards. The constable leapt madly to safety, falling headlong to the ground, and in a few seconds the car had whirled out of sight.

As Devenish climbed out of the Aston Martin he presented a picture which would last a long time in the minds of those who saw him.

His usually impeccably groomed hair was ruffled, his right cheek was smeared with blood from a slight wound just below his eye. His hands, swinging beside him unconcernedly, were a mass of cuts and scratches. His coat was ripped on the shoulder, and a piece of steel still lodged in the rent—but there was a twisted smile on his lips, and a glint in his eyes.

The constable stared.

'You're knocked about a bit, aren't you, sir? I . . . '

'It was a Chrysler that took the man away, wasn't it?' cut in Devenish.

The policeman nodded.

'Yes,' he agreed. 'I'd better be calling the Yard. Will you accompany me to the box, sir?'

'I will indeed,' said Devenish, grimly.

The policeman gave his report with admirable precision, answered one or two questions, then looked at Devenish, still holding the receiver.

'May I have your name, sir?' he inquired formally.

Devenish grinned and gave it.

'But,' he went on, before the man spoke into the mouthpiece. 'I'd like a word with a Mr. Fellowes. Do you think . . .?'

The constable looked impressed.

'You mean the Commissioner, Sir?'

'The Commissioner,' agreed Devenish.

'One moment, sir,' murmured the constable respectfully.

In a couple of minutes Hugh Devenish was talking to the Commissioner of Police at Scotland Yard.

'Hallo, Bill!' commenced Devenish breezily.

Commissioner William Fellowes grunted.

'It's you again, is it?' he demanded. 'I thought you'd gone native. What's the trouble?'

'Lots and lots,' grinned Devenish, 'of large men with little guns and a dislike of me.'

At the other end of the wire, Fellowes widened his eyes, and snapped out a request to a clerk who was with him to get the number of 'Z' Department.

'Hold the line a moment,' he told Devenish, then spoke into the other telephone on his desk.

A moment's conversation with Craigie sufficed him.

'So you're on that game, are you?' he said, back on the line to Devenish.

'By the grace of Providence and a pretty face,' said Hugh, 'I am. Tell this constable I can go, will you?'

Fellowes chuckled.

'Confound you—yes. But wait a moment, Hugh. Craigie wants to know when you're going round.'

'In a couple of hours, if I'm alive,' said Devenish cheerfully.

Twenty-five minutes later, he arrived at Companies House, went straight to the department of company registration, and soon had in front of him a pile of papers concerning the Marritaband Development Company Ltd.

At first sight, his mission looked like being disappointing. The Marritaband Development Company had gone out of existence two years before, apparently because there had been nothing left to develop. The unfortunates who had bought shares had lost everything they had invested.

As he made a note of the names of the four directors, he commented on his disappointment to the clerk who was helping him in his search.

The man scratched his forehead.

'If my memory serves me well,' he commented, 'I remember that the Marritaband Company, after its bankruptcy, was purchased by another firm—now let me see,' he muttered, closing his eyes with the effort of memory. 'I seem to remember a very great similarity of names—Marrit—Marritibar—no, that's not it, but the name's on the tip of my tongue, sir. I—I beg your pardon?'

He broke off, as Devenish snapped his fingers. Devenish had been leaning against a desk, gazing out of the window overlooking Waterloo Bridge, but as the name came to him he turned on the clerk with a gleam of excitement in his eyes.

'Marritibas!' he muttered. 'I thought as much. . ..'

The clerk quickly found the papers regarding Marritaba Tin Mines, Ltd., and Devenish turned to the original form of application, which held the names and addresses of the directors of the company.

There were four.

As Devenish had suspected, the directors of Marritaba Tin Mines, Ltd., had also been the directors of the Marritaband Development Company.

Exactly one hour after he had called at Companies House, Devenish walked thoughtfully back to his car. The names and addresses of all four directors of the two companies—one of which had ruined Tony Carruthers—in his pocket.

Before he set out on a tour of the four addresses, he telephoned Craigie.

'I want another three or four hours,' said Devenish, without preamble.

'For the love of Mike, be careful, Hugh. This job's getting nasty.'

'Did you say getting?' asked Devenish.

# 9

# DEVENISH MAKES SOME VISITS

The first name on the list of the Marritabas directors was Mr. Samuel Benjamin Martin, who lived at Queen's Court Chambers, Grosvenor Gardens, S.W.I. Devenish had no desire to meet Mr. Martin personally. He wanted, simply, to obtain a photograph of the director, who had shared in the prosecution of Marion Dare four years earlier.

A middle-aged charwoman opened the door. Mr. Martin, so she told him, would not be in until after six.

'What a pity,' sighed Devenish, unostentatiously putting his foot against the jamb.

As he spoke, he dipped his hand into his breast pocket, and with a quickness which did anything but deceive the woman's eye, he produced a pound note.

The woman opened the door more widely, eyeing the note.

'Please listen,' urged Devenish, stepping over the threshold into a tastefully furnished room which bespoke the success of Marritabas—for Mr. Martin. 'I don't want to steal anything. Find me one photograph of Martin, and this is yours. If I could have a look round,' he suggested helpfully, 'I expect I could find one. Does he keep a photograph album, do you know?'

The charwoman retreated into the room.

'Humph!' she snorted. 'I'd say 'e do. Alius being photographed with a girl, and alius a different girl. I don't know what the world's comin' to, that I don't.'

Devenish sighed.

'Nor do I,' he admitted sadly, looking round the room with considerable interest.

It was not overloaded with furniture, and besides a luxurious Chesterfield suite in blue tapestry, there were only two small bookcases half-filled with paperbacks, an occasional table, and a desk.

The woman opened the desk and pulled open an inner drawer. There were papers inside which it might have paid Devenish to study, but he had neither the time nor the opportunity. Had he started to read them, the charwoman would almost certainly have repented, and he had no desire to antagonise her.

At the back of the drawer was a small, leather-covered album, decorated in gold with S.B.M.—Mr. Martin's initials.

Devenish sorted through the little pack of postcard enlargements at the back of the book, glad that he would be able to take a photograph without leaving an empty space.

Martin was tall and well-built, with finely-cut features and dark heavily-lidded eyes. Not a man likely to be easily forgotten, Devenish thought, as he slipped one of the enlargements into his pocket and the pound note into the charwoman's eager hand. Then, with a cheery wave, he let himself out of the flat.

As he walked along the short corridor, from which two other flats opened, he heard heavy footsteps coming up the stairs. Settling his face into an expression of cheerful vacuity, Devenish walked on.

His expression very nearly let him down, as the newcomer turned into the passage. For Mr. Samuel Benjamin Martin was coming home much earlier than the charwoman had expected.

In the flesh, the director of Marritaba Tin was even more handsome than his photographs had predicted, but in his eyes there was, at that moment, an expression of ferocious anger which made Devenish thankful that the meeting had not taken place five minutes earlier. Martin was hurrying, and his arms swung vigorously at his sides.

Devenish, who had never been known to miss an opportunity, thought suddenly that he would have a still better knowledge of Samuel if he heard his voice. The idea came to him as they were level with each other—Martin had not troubled to look at Devenish, but walked on, glaring straight ahead.

'I wonder what's upset his apple cart?' Devenish thought to himself, and slipped sideways, cannoning into Martin's big frame. The man staggered away, banging his head hard against the wall.

Devenish recovered himself quickly.

'I say!' he exclaimed, with an apologetic expression of doelike dismay in his eyes, 'I'm sorry . . .'

Mr. Martin swung round, swearing viciously.

'You clumsy lout!' he snapped harshly. 'Why the hell don't you look where you're going?'

Devenish swallowed hard. At all times there were methods of expression which he disliked, and at this moment he disliked the man's tone, words, and manner.

'I said,' he murmured coldly, 'that I was sorry.'

'I'll teach you!' Martin grated, aiming a weighty but ill timed blow at Devenish's chin. 'I—ach!'

'That,' murmured Devenish brightly, as he shot his fist outwards, 'will teach you that all nice gentlemen accept an apology.'

The director of Marritabas crashed to the floor. He was stunned, but not unconscious, Devenish saw quickly, and was best left alone.

Mr. Horace Oswald Birch, the second director on Devenish's list, lived with his wife and child in Gomshall Gardens. Mrs. Birch turned out to be a faded, harassed-looking woman, struggling vainly to cope with the obstinacy of an unruly five-year-old.

He *did* want his photograph taken. And whatever his mother said, he was going to *have* it taken.

'But,' said the woman, with a helpless shrug, 'the gentleman doesn't want to *take* photographs, he wants to *copy* them. Ronald must. . .'

'Look here,' said Devenish, with his most captivating smile, 'I've a camera in my car. If you'll let me make you half a dozen copies of a family group, Mrs. . . . '

'Birch,' supplied Mrs. Birch.

'I'll do one of the youngster without charging. It means,' Hugh added convincingly, 'a great deal to me, madam. My firm specialises in enlargements, and unless I get a certain number of orders . . .'

Mrs. Birch surrendered, and Devenish took Ronald's picture, gave Ronald sixpence, and went away from the flat with a family group of the Birches in his pocket.

Mr. Honeybaum, the third director, lived in Chelsea's most residential quarter, near Cheyne Walk. The maid was very sorry, but she couldn't possibly let the gentleman have a photograph—no—really. . ..

'You know,' said Devenish, waggishly, 'I think you're afraid of what Mr. Honeybaum looks like. I. . .'

'Indeed I'm not!' asserted the maid vehemently. 'He's a very nice-looking gentleman.' She looked at Devenish, flushed with her championing and with the light of battle in her eyes. 'Why,' she went on, drawing back into the hall a pace—she had kept the caller on the well-whitened door-step—'there's a photo of him hanging here—you can see for yourself.'

Devenish craned his neck, thankful for even a sight of Mr. Honeybaum, who appeared to be a man of medium height, silver-haired and benevolent of aspect. He agreed that her loyalty was justified, and made his exit, a little disappointed, but realising that luck couldn't last for ever. At least he knew what the third director looked like.

The fourth and last director was Octavius William Young, whose name had after it: 'British-French origin.'

Mr. Young was the only member of the board who lived in the suburbs, his residence being in Mortimer Road, Barnes. His house was the proud possessor of a name, not a number, and was called 'Fourways'.

Devenish strode up to the front door, having left his car some distance up the road, and banged on the ornate iron knocker. The banging echoed inside the house, but there was no sound of movement. Devenish knocked again, and again, still without an answer.

He shrugged his shoulders and walked away. The place was empty, and he had no desire to make a forced entry. He strolled to the corner of Mortimer Road and looked back at 'Fourways', hoping that someone would turn into it.

The nearest house was fifty yards away, and three sides of the residence of Mr. Young faced common land.

As Devenish watched, a car turned off the road leading across the common, and into Mortimer Road. At first he noticed it casually; then he stiffened.

There might be nothing in it, he reasoned to himself; but the car was a Chrysler, twin brother to the rescue car of Clarges Street.

Devenish hunched his head into his shoulders and half turned, hoping that he was hidden from the view of the uniformed chauffeur, yet still contrived to watch the car. Suddenly he gave a start of surprise.

The driver was Marcus Riordon's ex-bruiser. The driver of the car which had tried to run him down the previous evening, and in all probability the driver of the car which had rescued his attacker that afternoon.

His eyes widened with astonishment as he saw the car draw up outside 'Fourways' and a man get out of the back passenger seat and walk rapidly towards the house.

Devenish whistled inaudibly. Of the many things which he had half-expected, he had never dreamed of finding Mr. Charles Rickett, secretary of the Carilon Club, visiting the home of one of Riordon's puppet directors.

# 10

# Lord Aubrey Chester Disappears

Devenish waited until the door had closed on Rickett and the Chrysler had been driven into the brick-built garage by the side of 'Fourways' before he moved towards his own car. He lost no time in getting into it, and left Mortimer Road quickly and with a prayer of devout thanks to the fates which had watched over him.

Apart from the indubitable danger, he was anxious, too, to get away knowing but unknown. He had learned many things that afternoon, all of which were interesting. Nothing, however, was of such vital importance to his mission for 'Z' Department as his discovery that Rickett was one of the workers in the Riordons' mysterious campaign.

As he hummed along the road towards Hammersmith, Devenish sat well back, his lips set firmly. He knew, now, why the death of Tony Carruthers had been such a complete mystery.

Knowing that, of course, was a long way from being able to prove it. On the other hand, Devenish was not concerned, directly, with the solving of Carruthers's murder. His job was a bigger one; and the part which Rickett was playing in the affair promised to reveal a line of investigation hitherto unknown.

The farther he went, the more certain he was that he had garnered a point which was invaluable, and he congratulated himself mildly on having resisted the temptation to have a go at the visitor to 'Fourways'.

As he said 'visitor' to himself, he wondered why.

Rickett had driven up to the house, had let himself in with a key, and his car had been garaged there. There was more than a chance, thought Devenish, that Mr.—known in the Press as 'M'sieu'—Rickett was none other than Octavius William Young (British-French origin).

The newspapers had reported that Rickett was partly French, on his mother's side. It was possible that he had been born in France, and it was equally possible that it had been a paternal, not maternal, French ancestry.

'In fact,' Devenish said to himself, as he hummed past Kensington Gardens, 'there's a lot about Mr. Rickett that I'd like to know. And I'm going to know—hallo!' He broke off, as a policeman stretched out a long arm towards him.

He pulled into the kerb, and the policeman came up to him.

'There's a call out for your car, sir. . . You *are* Mr. Devenish?'

'That's me.'

'The call,' explained the policeman, 'is from Headquarters, sir, and will you please ring up the usual place.'

'Thanks,' said Devenish, thoughtfully.

He climbed out of the car, and walked quickly to a telephone booth on the other side of the road. For the second time that day he heard Craigie's voice.

'Now what's the trouble?' demanded Devenish.

He heard Craigie's sharp exclamation.

'Are you all right?' demanded the Chief of 'Z' Department.

'So far as I know,' answered Devenish, frowning. 'Why?'

'Had any trouble?' asked Craigie.

'Not quite,' said Devenish, with a reminiscent smile. 'But why all the mystery, old son? What's the bother?'

'The bother,' said Craigie, grimly, 'started when the Yard got a message that you were finished. I. . .'

'Finished?' echoed Devenish weakly. 'You mean nailed up.'

'On the way to it,' said Craigie, 'an Aston Martin caught fire at Hampstead, and it had your number plate on. You— or at least,' corrected the Chief of 'Z' Department, with the ghost of a chuckle, 'your dummy, was burned beyond recognition.'

He paused.

'I'll be damned!' breathed Devenish.

'Well, it's a fake job, thank God. We'll talk about it later. When are you coming over?'

'Pretty soon,' said Devenish, 'just to prove I'm still alive.'

He replaced the receiver thoughtfully, and walked back to his car.

He was still thoughtful half an hour later, as he pulled up outside one of the big houses in Regent's Park. Among the things that had puzzled him more than he liked was Lord Aubrey Chester's appearance in the cream-coloured Bentley in the neighbourhood of Wharncliff Hall. Always providing, of course, that it *had* been Aubrey whom he had glimpsed.

A sober-visaged butler opened the door, and bowed solemnly as he went into the house.

He waited until the man had closed the door, then asked mildly for Aubrey.

The butler coughed deprecatingly.

'Lord Aubrey has not been in since early this morning, sir. But I think her ladyship is in. I will announce you.'

Devenish followed him across the hall. From either wall, portraits of Lord Aubrey's ancestors gazed sternly down. There were few things in this house which were not redolent of the fame of the Chesters.

Inside the wide, high-ceilinged drawing-room, Aubrey Chester's wife, Diane, was leaning back on a brocade-covered settee. They had been married just three years. Tall and slim, with dark, laughing eyes, Diane was well-known for her charm and gaiety. But now, as Devenish approached her, he saw at once that there was something wrong. She looked up at him anxiously as he took her hand.

'Hallo,' he said. 'Where's Aubrey?'

Diane shook her head.

'I don't know. I was hoping he was with you. He said he was going out for a spin . . .'

'What in?' asked Devenish.

'The Bentley. What do you know, Hugh?'

'I thought I saw him in the Horsham district this morning,' said Devenish. 'Was it a cream Bentley?'

'You do know something. What is it?'

Devenish shook his head regretfully.

'Nothing, apart from thinking I saw him in a cream-coloured Bentley this morning, scorching like blazes and. . .'

Diane sighed.

'I suppose he's all right,' she said. 'It's not like him, though, to go out for as long as this without phoning me. And he said he'd be back for lunch.'

Devenish leaned forward and tugged Diane's hair playfully.

'Well, you are a fuss-pot, I must say. But if you're really worried I'll make an inquiry or two—though heaven only knows what old Aubrey will say when he hears about it.'

'I wish you would,' said Diane eagerly.

Devenish moved to a telephone which was on a small table nearby, picked up the receiver and dialled the Yard. Although he was trying hard not to show it, he was in fact more than perturbed. Aubrey was too fond of his wife to worry her unnecessarily. Knowing the trouble that was in the air, and knowing that Aubrey had heard Riordon's fatal slip when he had given away his knowledge of how Curruthers had been murdered, Devenish was doubly anxious. And it was peculiar, to say the least of it, about the cream Bentley incident.

Nevertheless he smiled reassuringly at Diane as he asked first for the Chief Commissioner, who had gone home, and then for Superintendent Arthur Moore.

Moore knew him well, and answered his query quickly.

'I haven't heard a thing, Hugh, but I'll make sure. Just a minute . . .'

'If he doesn't know anything,' Devenish said to Diane, 'there's nothing to know. Hallo, Arthur—nothing reported? Be a good soul and try the Sussex and Hampshire people, will you?'

They waited for half an hour, before the Superintendent came through with a negative report.

'There you are,' said Devenish, chucking Diane under the chin. 'No smash. He'll turn up.'

But he was even more concerned when he left the house in Regent's Park, and drove back to his flat in Clarges Street.

# 11

# THE HON. MARCUS GETS CROSS

On the morning after he had met Hugh Devenish at the Carilon Club Lord Aubrey Chester had felt worried about the events of the night before. He felt that something was wrong, and that the something concerned Riordon Junior, and after thinking it over he saw the incident beneath the Admiralty Arch in its true light.

Consequently, a telegram purporting to come from Devenish, telephoned from the exchange, left him in no doubt as to his course of action.

The telegram was cleverly worded—by the Hon. Marcus.

*For the love of Mike* (it read) *hop down to Wharncliff Hall, Sussex, and ask for me.* And the signature was *Hugh.*

Aubrey, always anxious not to alarm Diane, had decided to say nothing to her about it, in the hope that he would be back for lunch, sent for the Bentley, and drove down to Wharncliff. To his surprise he was greeted by the Hon. Marcus Riordon, and he realised that he had been tricked.

'L-look here,' he stammered, 'I d-don't know what the g-game is, but. . .'

Marcus Riordon beamed brightly, but there was a gleam in his eyes that was the reverse of merriment.

'Don't you?' he inquired. 'Well—step in and see, Aubrey.'

'I'm d-damned if I will!' protested Chester fiercely. 'Where's Hughie, darn you?'

The Hon. Marcus casually slipped his hand into his pocket and brought out a small, dull grey automatic.

'Step in and see,' he insisted.

Aubrey's eyes dilated. He stood dead still.

'Y-you fool! Y-you can't get away with this . . .'

'I can try,' said Marcus, scowling suddenly. 'Get in, blast you!'

He jabbed the gun into his visitor's ribs, and Chester had no choice but to obey.

Wharncliff Hall was as magnificently furnished as the house in Regent's Park, but rather more sombre. Stepping nervously between grinning tigers and an occasional snarling panther, Aubrey went on, the gun still prodding his ribs. The Hon. Marcus turned into a small room, barely furnished, and lit, although it was morning, with electric light.

Aubrey blinked about him and noticed that there were no windows.

'Sit down!' ordered the Hon. Marcus, shoving the other into one of two leather-covered arm-chairs. 'You'll get some food—if you behave—and if you keep quiet.'

He turned on his heel. Aubrey heard the key turn in the lock, and realised that he was as safely imprisoned as he would have been in Dartmoor.

There was no expression of benevolence on Marcus Riordon's face when he spoke to the three men who sat with him at a small table in an upstairs room at Wharncliff Hall.

His eyes glittered, and there was a cruel twist on his face, which seemed thinner than usual. From the tubby, genial little man whom the members of the Carilon Club, amongst others, knew so well, the Hon. Marcus seemed to have grown into a man of deep, evil power.

Had Hugh Devenish seen him at that time, he would have immediately recognised Riordon's unquestioned air of leadership. The three men with him were obviously subordinates. Riordon stood, figuratively, head and shoulders above them.

On his right side was Samuel Benjamin Martin, sullen-faced, obviously squirming beneath Riordon's anger. Martin played with the stub of a pencil all the time Riordon spoke, and he lit cigarette after cigarette, chain fashion.

Between Martin and the third man was Sir Basil Riordon. He sat hunched up in his chair, more gaunt and wizened than ever; his eyes, normally glittering and alert, were lifeless. He said nothing, unless in reply to a direct question, and from time to time he removed his gaze away from his son, staring at a little packet in the middle of the polished, otherwise empty, table.

Next to the financier was Octavius William Young— sometimes known as Charles Rickett, secretary of the Carilon Club. His dark face was expressionless, and his eyes were narrowed, inscrutable. Of the three, Rickett seemed the only one capable of standing against the Hon. Marcus.

Marcus Riordon stopped speaking for a moment, and lit a cigarette which he stuck carefully into his long holder.

The three men waited without speaking.

Marcus puffed a stream of blue-grey smoke into the air, and looked coldly at Martin.

'Well,' he said evenly. 'You've nothing to say, have you?'

Martin's dark eyes glinted in repressed anger.

'What can I say?' he grunted. 'I—slipped up, Riordon. What's done can't be undone.'

'What you mean,' said the Hon. Marcus bitingly, 'is that you haven't the brains to put it right, blast you! That move with the Aston Martin was perfect, and you . . . ' he broke off with a high-pitched, mirthless laugh—'you worked it a day too soon. Tomorrow we'd have had Devenish here— and the police would have thought he'd been burnt to death.'

'Supposing you don't manage to get hold of Devenish?' muttered Martin. 'He's not easy . . . '

'I'll look after that part of it,' snapped Riordon savagely.

'You'll have to,' retorted Martin. 'Anyhow. I could have *sworn* the note you sent said today . . . '

Riordon's eyes flashed viciously.

'You'd swear black was blue, to save your skin,' he snarled. 'You'd better be more careful in future, Martin, or . . . '

He left the sentence unfinished, but Martin flinched as though something had cut into his skin.

The Hon. Marcus turned away from him, and looked cruelly at his father's huddled figure.

'As for you,' he said in a curiously flat voice, 'I reckon you'd be better out of the way. All you had to do was keep the girl here, and you let Devenish get her.'

Sir Basil stared dully. Then his gaze dropped to the packet on the table. The Hon. Marcus sneered.

'That's all you think about,' he said cruelly. 'Fill you up with snow, and you're happy . . . '

The old man stirred. His lips twitched.

'I must have it!' he pleaded desperately. 'I must, Marcus! Where would you be without me?'

'I'll show you one day.'

Sir Basil's eyes blazed for a moment, then went dull. Cocaine—or 'snow', as Marcus called it—kept him alive. Without it he was a hopeless, senile wreck. His son controlled his supplies very carefully. There were times when the old man's financial genius was necessary, and then Marcus doled out the drug generously. At others, the financier went for days without it, his mind and body wracked, his son watching him callously in his torment.

Rickett leaned forward and spoke in his even voice, with curiously clipped sentences.

'You'd better let him feed,' he said. 'He needs it.'

The Hon. Marcus sneered.

'Since when have you been leading this outfit?' he asked sarcastically. 'You put Devenish on to it, damn you!'

Rickett returned the other's stare without flinching. It was true, of course, that he had made a bad slip, when killing Carruthers. The puncture in Carruthers's neck instead of his arm had precluded any possibility of suicide.

Rickett did not know that it was Marcus who had first awakened Hugh Devenish's suspicions—and Riordon, confident though he was in his ability to control the others, felt a sneaking satisfaction at that. Rickett's imperturbability disturbed him perhaps more than he admitted to himself; Rickett was deep.

Rickett shrugged his shoulders.

'What is—is,' he said. 'But the old man needs snow. He's got work—tomorrow.'

The Hon. Marcus swallowed hard, and took the little packet between his fingers. It was no time now to quarrel with Rickett, and it was true enough that the old man had an important part to play in the carefully-planned plot.

He tossed the packet across the table. Sir Basil clawed at it pitifully, his eyes glistening, his whole body quivering. Tearing at the paper with shaking, feverish hands, he poured a little of the powder it contained on to his palm and threw it into his mouth. Then he dropped back in his chair like a dead man. Inside ten minutes, the others knew, he would be like a man resurrected, keen-eyed, alert.

Rickett took a long, thin cigarette from a silver case and lit it.

'What's the next move?' he asked.

The Hon. Marcus narrowed his eyes.

'We've got to get Devenish,' he said, with an edge to his voice, 'and we've got to get the girl back. She knows too much to be healthy.'

'What if she's already talked?' queried Rickett.

Riordon's lips twisted; for a moment he looked what Marion Dare thought him—the cruellest man in the world.

'If she has,' he muttered, 'I'll flay her alive! For God's sake, Rickett, don't keep *making* trouble.'

There was a flicker of scorn in Rickett's eyes, but it passed in a moment.

'You think Devenish will come—after Chester?'

'He will, if I know Devenish,' said Marcus craftily. 'When he's here, we'll get the girl back.'

'And then?' queried Rickett, watching a smoke-ring disappear into the haze above the four men.

Marcus tapped his fingers against the side of his chair in a ceaseless tattoo.

'Then,' he said softly, 'we can start using Bleddon's.'

# 12

# BLEDDON'S BANK

The general manager of Bleddon's Bank was a much worried man. Of recent years, the responsibility of the tremendous undertaking had rested more and more upon his shoulders, and if he could have controlled the thousand-and-one activities of the bank from start to finish, it was more than likely that he would have made a good job of it. Unfortunately, his control was limited. He did as he was told by Sir Basil Riordon; his income depended on so doing.

On the morning of the fifteenth of September, he sat in his sumptuously furnished office and brooded. The Governing Director—Sir Basil—was due at the magnificent headquarters of Bleddon's—situated in Lombard Street—and Macauly—the general manager—had a disturbing feeling that he would get instructions which he would be unable to view with a favourable eye.

For more years than Macauly had lived, Bleddon's had been the peak of banking. Its branches spread over the whole of the civilised world, its credit was inviolable, its honesty and fair dealing irreproachable. Nothing was more solid, in the mind of the Great British Public, than Bleddon's Bank.

No breath of scandal had ever been raised against it, and it was the only remaining private bank—its shares were not on the market, but were controlled by Sir Basil Riordon and a host of smaller directors who knew as well as Macauly that they were Riordon's puppets.

Even the Marritaba failure had brought no hornets about the ears of Bleddon's. Macauly knew that the bank had really floated the shares—or Riordon had, which was the same thing—but this knowledge was not general.

If Macauly could have believed that Marritabas were just one bad break in a long series of successful ones, he would have shrugged his shoulders and admitted that all men made mistakes. But he did not believe that. He suspected— more by inference and a knowledge of Riordon's character than by any direct information—that Riordon had deliberately rigged the market.

The very thought made Macauly go hot and cold. If the G.B.P. once got a whisper of that, there would be such a run on Bleddon's as there had never been on a single bank in the history of economic finance. The result would be catastrophic.

At half past eleven an electric buzzer on his desk warned Macauly that Sir Basil had arrived, and was stepping out of his car. In time-honoured fashion the general manager hurried out of his office towards the great revolving doors of the main entrance and stood on the pseudo-marble steps to welcome the Governing Director.

He did not notice the three well-dressed men who were lounging outside the bank, for the simple reason that he was too intent on greeting Riordon. Had he noticed them, he would have found it hard to reconcile the men's immaculate dress with their hard, brutal faces and watchful eyes glittering with that flintiness peculiar to the killer.

As the two bank officials shook hands, the three loungers quietly closed in on the main entrance, their right hands thrust deep into their coat pockets.

Sir Basil, thought Macauly, was looking better in health than he had for some time. The financier's eyes were bright, and there was a slight flush of colour on his cheeks; he looked less gaunt than usual.

Macauly felt more hopeful than he had ten minutes before.

'Glad to see you looking so well, sir,' he said, as Riordon was ushered through the door by a respectful commissionaire.

Sir Basil shrugged his shoulders.

'I'm getting old, you know, Macauly. I can't last for ever—got to make room for these younger fellows, I'm afraid.'

As the doors closed behind the two men, the three loungers outside converged on the bank. A large touring Daimler drew smoothly and silently into the kerb and, as it pulled up, the chauffeur, a flat-faced, brutal-looking man with colossal shoulders, sent the electric siren on the car screeching into the air.

A dozen passers-by looked round, startled.

They saw the three gangsters make a sudden dash through the door and heard a sudden babble of voices from inside the bank, a woman's scream quivering high above them.

Through the half-closed door came a high-pitched cry of pain. The door flew open, forced by the dead weight of the commissionaire, who fell headlong into the street, his face ashen grey, blood pouring from an ugly wound in his neck.

Inside the bank, a dozen cashiers stood behind the grilles, their eyes distended in terror, their hands held stiffly above their heads. In a fraction of a second four tight-lipped men who had been inside the bank for five minutes past, on the pretext of business, had moved towards the counter; ugly, snub-nosed automatics pointed threateningly at the terrified clerks.

Macauly saw the attack, realising in sudden horror what it meant. Yet it seemed macabre, unreal.

Two of the gunmen jumped swiftly on to the counter and over the grille. Holding their guns in their right hands, they grabbed packet after packet of treasury notes, throwing them into a valise which one of them had left on the other side of the grille.

'My God!' cried Macauly. 'We must. . .'

As he started to speak, he moved forward, forgetting Riordon in the urgency of the moment. White-faced, he leapt at the nearest gunman.

The man snarled viciously and touched the trigger of his gun. Bullets spattered out, with little zutts! telling of silenced automatics, and Macauly reared, staggered, then dropped heavily to the floor.

The little crowd of men and women in the bank stood staring in horror. A woman screamed, another collapsed in a heap on the floor, while the four gunmen, working with the speed of lightning, filled the valise. Three more gun-men—those whom Macauly had seen but not noticed out-side—stood by the door, their guns trained threateningly on the stupefied clerks.

One of them rasped out a command.

'That's enough!' he snapped. 'Beat it, all of you!'

The gangsters acted on the instant. The two on the inside of the counter vaulted up and over the grille, grabbed the valise, snapped it shut and threw it to the men by the door, who caught it dexterously and disappeared.

The others backed towards the door, holding their guns in front of them. Apart from the one command, none of them had spoken. They moved quickly, silently, but there was the threat of death in their eyes for anyone who tried to interrupt them. The great building was filled with a low, barely audible surge of sound as the tension of the men and women inside it slowly relaxed, but the shadow of that awful death seemed still to stupefy them.

The last of the gunmen slipped out of the door, and as he went, Sir Basil Riordon, who had crouched back against the wall throughout the attack, staring down at the huddled body of the general manager, fell forward in a dead faint. A cashier, the first to force himself out of the paralysing grip of the outrage, ran towards him. He seemed to release the others, as though he had galvanised them into action. In a moment, clerks, cashiers, and customers made bedlam, pushing, jostling and shouting.

Outside, the gunmen streaked towards the waiting Daimler and another car which slid behind it, leaping over the still body of the commissionaire.

A policeman, whose whistle had been blasting for the past two minutes, bringing a rush of people towards Bleddon's Bank, made a determined but foolhardy rush at the foremost gangster. Two yards away from his quarry he threw up his arms, spun round, and fell to the pavement.

Someone screamed. A well-dressed man, carrying an attaché-case, hurled it towards the killers, shouting at the top of his voice and rushing forward. Once again the gunmen fired.

Then the raiders crammed themselves into the two cars, which slid into motion.

As they moved, half a dozen policemen converged on them, hurling their truncheons in a forlorn hope of hitting the drivers, but another rattle of firing drove them back. The cars surged forward at a tremendous pace, accelerating with the sudden power of super-charged engines, and in thirty seconds they had disappeared from sight.

And then bedlam was let loose in Lombard Street.

# 13

# Hugh Devenish Gets a Message

In the carefully-guarded room at Whitehall, known to a select few as 'Z' Department, Gordon Craigie sat in an easy chair, listening to Hugh Devenish.

Devenish looked worried, and there was a furrow of anxiety on his forehead. He smoked incessantly, and picked his words with more care than usual.

'I know it sounds fantastic,' he said doggedly, 'but it's my opinion, Gordon, and all the flatfoots in the world won't make me alter it. That raid on Bleddon's was staged by Riordon.'

Craigie took his meerschaum from his thin lips.

'It *is* a tall story,' he commented non-committally.

'It's all a tall story,' retorted Devenish. 'From start to finish—as far as we've got, anyway—it's been a nightmare. Tony Carruthers was murdered, and the only reason we can see for it is fear that he might have told someone who it was who advised him to buy Marritabas. Remember, we *know* Riordon, the son, was concerned with Carruthers . . .'

'We don't,' protested Craigie. 'We only guess he was.'

'I'm not talking logic and rule of thumb,' Devenish said, 'I'm talking horse-sense. Riordon let slip the "neck" business and tried to kill me afterwards.'

'He might have done both,' said Craigie. 'On the other hand, the running down business at the Admiralty Arch might have had nothing to do with Riordon.'

'It was his chauffeur, darn you!' snapped Devenish irritably. 'Stop being cussed, and listen to reason. We know, near enough, that Riordon was behind Carruthers's murder, and we know that he's been doing some funny business down at Wharncliff Hall.'

'We've only got the girl's word for that,' said Craigie cautiously.

Devenish snapped his fingers.

'Marion Dare's word is good enough for me,' he said decisively. 'This is how I see it, Gordon. The Riordons, father and son, are behind Marritabas, and Marritabas is one of the biggest swindles we've had for a long time. Carruthers was murdered because he could have given a clue that the Riordons were behind it. If Bleddon's Bank was concerned at all, Macauly probably knew as much as Carruthers. So Macauly had to be put away as well. Is that logical?'

'It's all right,' admitted Craigie, cautiously.

'Thank the Lord for that!' muttered Devenish, crossing one leg over the other and settling back in his chair. 'Now it's reasonable, too, that there mustn't be a chance of connecting the murder of Macauly with Riordon. If he'd simply been bumped off, the police would have put two and two together and the Riordons would have been in queer street. So they staged the hold-up, calculating that the police would never link the raid on Bleddon's with Sir Basil, who virtually owns the bank.

'Remember,' he went on, as Craigie stirred, 'Marcus might know that I, and even the police, suspect him of being concerned with Carruthers, but he can't know that we believe he's hand in glove with his father. That's the strong point of my reckoning. Riordon senior is still above suspicion, and visits the bank for a conference with his general manager, who invariably meets his boss on the bank steps. Now we're all set. The ruse is to make us believe the raid, coinciding with Riordon's visit, was accidental. Actually, the raid was timed when it was known Macauly would be on view. The actual robbery, the shooting, was just a blind, to make us believe that Macauly was killed more or less because he was in the way, instead of being killed because he was as dangerous to the Riordons as Carruthers was. And,' went on Devenish grimly, 'from what I can gather, no one apart from myself doubts that Macauly's murder was incidental. Even you , . .'

Craigie interrupted.

'I'm only giving you the official point of view,' he said. 'Nobody, so far, thinks I'm right about Sir Basil Riordon— they all think I've a bee in my bonnet. Even Bill Fellowes— though Bill does admit that things look bad against the Hon. Marcus.'

Devenish gave a brief, one-sided opinion on the mentality of the Police Commissioner. 'All right,' said Craigie, with a fleeting grin, 'Bill might be all that, but he'll still take a lot of persuading that the bank raid was staged just to kill Macauly. So will the Home Secretary. And before we can get them to move at all seriously, we've got a great deal to prove, Hugh.'

'A raid on Wharncliff Hall would prove a lot of things,' growled Devenish.

'At the moment,' said Craigie, 'it wouldn't be justified. Before we could do it, we'd have to get the nearest thing to Cabinet approval that we know—and for the time being we couldn't show reason for it. All the same,' he added, tapping the bowl of his pipe against the bars of the grate, 'I'd like to see the inside of Wharncliff Hall.'

Devenish cocked an eye at his Chief.

'You mean I ought to have a shot at it?'

'I mean,' said Craigie carefully, 'that I'll let you have half a dozen men to do what you like with, Hugh, but on the usual terms. It'd be unofficial. Riordon senior may be unpopular because he has kept quiet recently, but he's still got a lot of influence.'

Devenish's eyes glistened. He knew, better than any man, the peril of working for 'Z' Department, and in this particular case, when he was pulling hard against police opinion, an unofficial raid on Wharncliff Hall with negligible results would undoubtedly land him in queer street.

On the other hand, he was convinced that the affair was coming rapidly to a head. At the moment he constituted an acute danger to Riordon, and it was as much by luck as by judgement that he was still alive to shout about it.

Whatever the Riordons were planning, they could not bring it off until he was put away. They dared not—he knew too much, and guessed more. It was a duel between himself and the Riordons' organisation—and there would be no quarter, no time lost.

In consequence he jumped at Craigie's offer of unofficial support. There were a dozen young, alert, seemingly indolent but actually energetic young men ready to take a chance on anything hectic that he, or 'Z' Department, could put in their way.

But before he acted he wanted to learn more of the two directors of the Marritiband Development Company. Octavius William Young and Samuel Benjamin Martin were well worth immediate attention.

He threw a half-finished cigarette into the fire, and leaned forward, tapping Craigie's knee.

'I'll take a chance, Gordon—and you can kick me if it goes wrong. By the way,' he added, leaning back in his chair, 'did you get any more news about the Aston Martin smash?'

Craigie smoothed his chin thoughtfully.

'Not much,' he said, 'but I persuaded Bill Fellowes to have a look at the wreckage before they carted the poor devil who was burned up to the mortuary. And—' Craigie leaned forward with a grim expression in his eyes— 'Fellowes told me that he could have sworn it was you.'

Devenish whistled.

'Did he, then! And even that doesn't make him see sense?'

'All that it did,' said Craigie, with a grimace, 'was to convince him that you've hit a hornets' nest somewhere. He isn't prepared to admit that the hornets' nest is Sir Basil.'

'All right, all right,' said Devenish, with an airy wave of his arm. 'We'll let it pass. Now listen to this. . ..'

Craigie listened intently while his agent related the story of his canvassing for photographic enlargements.

'You're getting hot,' he admitted, when Devenish had finished. 'Rickett wants watching.'

'That'll be a job for the army you're giving me,' said Devenish cheerfully. 'Who is it to be, Gordon?'

'I'll send all six of them to the Carilon Club at nine o'clock,' Craigie said. 'If I can get hold of them all, that is. You'll know them, Hugh.'

'That suits me,' said Devenish, feeling more cheerful than he had done since the news of the bank raid and the merciless killing had reached him two days before.

He heaved himself out of the chair.

'Well,' he said, patting Craigie on the shoulder, 'I'll be going.'

Craigie did not smile. He knew that Devenish was preparing to take the biggest risk of his life.

Hugh Devenish made his way through devious routes until he reached Whitehall, and eventually found himself in the courtyard of Scotland Yard.

A tall, middle-aged man, exquisitely turned out and walking with a peculiar thrust forward on his right foot, was coming down the steps of the building as Devenish reached the foot of them.

'Hallo, Bill,' greeted Devenish. 'How are you?'

The Police Commissioner smiled. He had a face, Devenish had once assured him, that had been incubated in an ice box. The features were regular rather than good, always set in the same cold expression, as though completely disbelieving everything that he was being told. The expression was affected, not characteristic, for William Fellowes had a keen, if dry, sense of humour, coupled with an ability to reach the essentials of a situation quickly and surely.

'I'm all right,' Fellowes said dryly, 'excepting when I'm being pestered by a wagon-load of loonies with a fantastic idea that. . .'

'Less of the loonies,' grinned Devenish. 'We're on a hot job, Bill, and all the flat-foots in London won't make us drop it.'

'Then mind your step,' warned Fellowes. 'Marcus Riordon might be a bad lot, but the old man's all right.'

'There are times,' said Devenish rudely, 'when I wonder what you've got behind your thick skull. When I've got everything worked out in simple arithmetic, I'll have another shot at convincing you.'

Fellowes chuckled.

'And I've warned you,' he said. 'Mind your step. You've hit a packet of trouble, Hugh, and you're working it from the wrong end. I'll give you one hint,' he said, as his car drew up to the kerb.

'If it's anything like your general conversation this morning,' grinned Devenish, 'I don't want it.'

'Take it or leave it,' commented Fellowes as he sat back in the car and the chauffeur pressed the self-starter. 'Be careful if you meet a lady called Lydia Crane. She's a friend of Marcus Riordon.'

Devenish assimilated this item of information as he walked briskly towards his flat. Lydia Crane. Surely that was the name Marion Dare had mentioned.

When he reached the flat, Marion had just returned from a shopping expedition with Pincher's married sister. Devenish had insisted on advancing the girl enough money to fit herself out with necessities until she could get her clothes from Wharncliff Hall.

A pleasant odour of grilling steak assailed Hugh's nostrils, and through the open door of the living-room he could hear Pincher arguing resignedly with his sister on the way in which onions should be fried. Occasionally the pugilistic Wiggings's voice came through.

Devenish threw himself in a chair and grinned at Marion Dare.

'The family'll get bad-tempered before we're much older,' he chuckled. 'Feeling all right, Marion?'

She smiled warmly.

'Thanks to you,' she said.

'Anything happened of interest?'

'I don't think so,' said Marion. 'Not here, anyhow.'

Devenish stuffed his pipe thoughtfully.

'By the way,' he said quietly, 'what can you tell me about Lydia Crane?'

He saw Marion's eyes cloud over.

'Marcus Riordon's friend,' she said.

'The regular visitor to Wharncliff?' queried Hugh.

'Yes.'

'What's she like to look at?'

Marion gave a brief but vivid description, and Devenish had little fear of not recognising the exotic Lydia Crane should he meet her.

It was more than interesting, he thought, that the Police Commissioner had warned him of the woman—Fellowes obviously knew something of Marcus Riordon's activities.

'It beats me,' said Hugh, who had slipped into the habit of discussing sidelights on the affair with Marion, 'that the police won't believe Sir Basil's a bad boy. If they know about the Crane woman they must know Marcus spends a lot of his time at the Hall.'

Marion looked worried.

'Perhaps they don't want to believe Sir Basil's mixed up in it,' she suggested evenly.

Devenish looked at her sharply.

'You mean—graft?'

Marion nodded.

'Yes. Riordon knows almost everybody who matters, from the Home Secretary downwards. I used to write to him regularly.'

'What about?' snapped Devenish, wide-eyed.

'Just little things—I wondered, sometimes, whether. . .'

She broke off uncertainly.

'Wondered what?'

'I don't know anything definitely,' said Marion, 'but there didn't seem any need for the letters unless they were a code of some kind.'

Devenish leaned back in his chair, frowning. All things were possible, of course, even graft on a grand scale in England. But the thought that Riordon was buying security from close investigation of his affairs needed more than a pinch of salt to make it palatable. The more he thought over the situation, however, the more he disliked the look of things.

But there was no need to worry Marion unduly. .

She looked up at him.

'I wish to goodness,' she said vehemently, 'that we could go away somewhere until it's all over!'

Devenish looked at her quizzically.

'Did you say we?'

Marion coloured a little. Devenish went over to her, and rested his hands on her slim shoulders.

'Did you?' he insisted.

Marion nodded almost imperceptibly.

'Then,' said Devenish, slipping one arm round her waist, 'I've a lot of things to say to you.'

They must have been pleasant, for when Pincher entered the room ten minutes later he was surprised to see Devenish sitting on the arm of Marion's chair—and their heads were very close together.

Devenish telephoned Craigie after lunch and arranged for two agents to keep an eye on 'Fourways', in Barnes, and two more to watch the movements of Rickett—*alias,* so Devenish believed, Octavius Young—and Samuel Benjamin Martin.

'Where are you going?' Craigie asked him.

'I need a rest,' Devenish lied glibly. 'You're sending the boys to the Carilon at nine, aren't you?'

'Hm-hm,' agreed the chief of 'Z' Department.

'I'll wait till then before I start again,' said Hugh, grinning at his thoughts.

He replaced the receiver and went into the sitting-room, where Marion was amusing herself with a Butterick fashion book.

'I was wondering,' said Hugh, 'whether you would graciously give me your company for an hour this afternoon. There's a very attractive little tea-room. . .'

They didn't hurry—a fact which Devenish bitterly regretted when they eventually returned to the flat.

Pincher, with an unerring instinct for the momentous, manœuvred his employer away from Marion.

'I don't know whether you would like Miss Dare to learn of this,' the valet said discreetly, 'but a lady called to see you an hour ago. She refused to give her name, but I had the impression, sir, that her call was not unconnected with the—er—affair on which you are spending so much time. She left this note . . . '

Devenish took the letter which Pincher slid from his pocket and slit the envelope open. From the paper, he knew that his caller had written her message in the flat.

'What was she like?' he demanded, scanning the note quickly.

Pincher turned his lips downwards in disapproval.

'She was what one might call, without being dramatic, *exotic,* Mr. Devenish. Tall, and of majestic proportions. I thought that she. . .'

Pincher was about to say that he opined that the caller had been of foreign nationality, but he stopped abruptly, for Devenish cursed with sudden and unexpected vehemence.

'Ring round for the car,' snapped Devenish, 'and tell them to have it here in ten minutes.'

He hurried into his bedroom as he spoke, and Pincher, who knew his moods perfectly, saw that he had had a jar, and a nasty one. Devenish's eyes were narrowed and the glint in them was like steel. His lips were pressed together in a grim line.

He rapidly gathered his 'tools', strapping them to his body with the dexterity of long practice, and slipped a loaded automatic into his pocket.

Hurrying out of the room he came face to face with Marion. The expression in his eyes made her start in alarm.

'What's happened?' she asked tensely.

Devenish showed her the note without speaking. As she read it her face paled.

In the round sloping hand of the woman whom she knew as Lydia Crane, although it was unsigned, was the brief, blunt statement that unless Devenish appeared, in person and alone, at Wharncliff Hall within the next three hours, the body of Lord Aubrey Chester would be found in London before midnight.

# 14

# TROUBLE AT WHARNCLIFF HALL

**M**arion handed back the note tight-lipped.

'You're going?' she asked, although she knew what his answer would be.

Devenish nodded.

'If I'm not back before nine,' he said quietly, 'telephone this number, and tell the man who answers you to send help to Wharncliff. He'll know what I mean.'

Afterwards he was thankful that he had given Marion Craigie's telephone number, although she did not obey his instructions to the letter.

It was six o'clock when Hugh Devenish left the Clarges Street flat, and it was a quarter to seven when he pulled up outside the doors of the Bull Inn after a whirlwind drive over fifty miles of good-to-middling roads. That a dozen startled constables had made a guess—they could not be sure—at his number worried him not at all.

He knew enough of the Riordons to believe that they would act on their threat—and he would have risked many things for Lord Aubrey Chester.

The landlord of the Bull recognised him immediately, and acceded without question to a request for a quiet if brief talk.

'Do you want to earn quick money?' asked Devenish. 'It's risky.'

'I'll take a chance, sir.'

'Good man!' breathed Devenish. 'I want to run this car into your shed, and I want you to lock the door and keep it locked until I come back. Is that clear?'

'I've got that,' said the man, pulling a bunch of keys from his pocket. 'And the next, sir?'

'That's the lot, for the time being,' said Devenish, 'and if anyone gets an idea what you're hiding, you're in for more trouble than you know.'

He ran the car into the shed, and obtained a lucid direction to Wharncliff Hall, using the lane along which Marion Dare had walked three mornings before. Giving the landlord a fiver, he started the last lap of his journey.

It was still daylight, although heavy clouds were spreading across the sky and casting a dark shadow over the countryside. Devenish swung along the lane, walking with long strides which covered the ground at considerable speed, taking careful note of his route as he went.

The first mile was easy enough to negotiate, for the lane was bordered on both sides by thickly-growing bramble bushes, and ran straight, without any turnings. At the end of the mile, however, the land ended in a meadow, and the rest of the journey to Wharncliff Hall was across downland.

Even without the well-trodden footpath, Devenish would have been able to make a bee-line for the Hall. He could see its grim outline clearly against the grey sky, a squat, ugly building, set in a vale between two hills.

No sound came to him as he strode on, beyond the whispering of a thousand creatures of the fields, and the occasional whine of a gust of wind sweeping from the south. Once he heard the low, threatening rumble of distant thunder, and far away to the right the blackening clouds were forked with a vivid yellow streak.

He had no doubt at all as to the danger into which he was walking. The Riordons wanted him dead, and they would take all manner of risks to get rid of him. But there was one risk, Devenish believed, which they would not take—and he thought that he could bluff them into believing it existed.

It was not his first gamble with death; but it was very likely the most dangerous.

He walked on towards the Hall, a peculiar gleam in his eyes, a puckish twist on his lips. Anyone watching his expression would have judged that he was looking forward to the next hour—and they would have been right.

The storm clouds raced across the sky, with thunder rumbling nearer and occasional streaks of lightning splitting the heavens in two. No rain came, but the wind grew in strength, blowing behind him with the force of a hurricane, sending the leaves swirling down from the trees about him.

Probably, Devenish thought, the storm was keeping the Riordons' underlings inside. As he approached the Hall he saw no one, and only in one window, on the second floor, was there a light. Without hesitating, he stepped from the fields across which he had walked into the garden of Wharncliff Hall. The grounds were neglected, he noticed. The grass on the wide lawns was uncut, and the rows of bushes had not been clipped for many months.

The front door of the Hall was approached by a short flight of steps, bordered by high, granite pillars.

Devenish was half-way up the steps when he had his first half-anticipated surprise.

The big, oak door swung open, without a moment's warning, and at the same moment the hall lights flared up, dazzling, blinding him! He stopped dead still, narrowing his eyes against the light. Before he could see the men in front of him a voice rapped out.

'Keep your hands in sight, Devenish!'

Devenish grinned blandly, and stepped forward.

'Well, well, well!' he drawled, peering into the hall, 'if dear old Marcus hasn't got another voice.'

The Hon. Marcus Riordon stood in the hall, scowling, with an armed man on each side of him.

'You won't feel so chirpy in a minute,' he rasped. 'Frisk him, you two.'

The two gunmen stepped forward, readily. In the threshold of the hall, Devenish stopped dead still and waited for them—and as he looked he grinned.

'Well, well, well!' he drawled again, 'if you haven't brought Rogers and Huggett to guard you—two boys who ought to know better . . .'

He spoke the last words very slowly, but there was an edge to his voice which made the men hesitate for a split second. They were the two who had been struggling with Marion Dare, three mornings before, and Devenish recognised them.

He let the two men run their hands over his body, as far as his thighs, gazing mockingly into Riordon's face the while. Rogers felt the automatic in his coat pocket, grabbing at it with a snort of satisfaction.

As the gun came out, Devenish swung both arms round with concentrated force. His clenched fists caught the unfortunate gangsters beneath the chin within a fraction of a second of each other, and both men went sprawling. As they fell, Devenish hurled his twelve stone of bone and muscle forward. Marcus staggered backwards, and Devenish whipped a second automatic from his trouser pocket, leapt back to the door, and covered his men easily.

It had all happened in the space of ten seconds.

Devenish closed the door with his free hand, still training his gun threateningly, and flashed a swift glance round the big, magnificently furnished hall. Directly ahead of him was a wide, curving staircase, thickly carpeted, leading to a second floor on which he could see three closed doors. On his right, he could see into a library, on his left another door was closed, leading into one of the front rooms. A wide, panelled passage led beyond the foot of the staircase to the right, ending at a heavy tapestry curtain. To the left of the passage, beneath the stairs, was a door leading into the room without windows—Aubrey Chester's recent prison, but this Devenish did not yet know.

Looking at the doors, he saw that there were four directions from which reinforcements could come—from upstairs, from the rooms to the right and left (there were probably doors leading out of them away from the hall) and from the rear of the hall, beyond the tapestry curtain.

But with his back to the front door, Devenish could see them all. There was little chance of a surprise attack.

On the other hand, he admitted freely that his advantage might well be only short-lived. If half a dozen or more of Riordon's roughnecks rushed him at once, he would be overwhelmed. It behove him to act, and talk, quickly.

He looked evenly at the Hon. Marcus.

'So you've got Aubrey here, have you?' he opened tentatively.

Riordon was beginning to recover his wits, and there was an evil glitter in his eyes.

'And I've got you here,' he said sneeringly. 'You won't get out so easily as you got in.'

'I don't intend to get out easily,' said Devenish softly.

'You won't. . .' began Riordon, but Devenish cut him short.

'Because,' he pointed out, 'I shall take Aubrey with me, and I've an idea that you will object.'

Riordon made a big effort to control his temper.

'I shall object, all right,' he said tightly. 'You're in a hole, Devenish, smart though you think you are.'

'Not smart!' implored Devenish. 'Clever, if you like, but *not* smart. Now, Rogers,' he went on, as the tougher of the two gangsters struggled into a sitting position on the floor, 'no games, in case this gun goes off.'

Rogers stood up, swearing beneath his breath.

'I'll get you . . .' he started, but Devenish stopped him.

'You told me that yesterday,' he said, 'or whenever it was I saw you last. Keep quiet, my friend, and look after Huggett—he needs looking after.'

Riordon moved back against the marble of the huge fireplace. His flabby face was pale.

'You can't get away with this,' he said harshly. 'I've got a dozen men in the house, and others outside. I. . .'

'I don't care how many men you've got,' said Devenish. 'I came to get Chester, and I'll get him. And I'm taking him away with me.'

'And what am I going to do while you're taking him?' sneered Riordon.

He half turned, and slid his right hand into his trouser pocket. Devenish appeared not to notice it.

'I don't know,' he drawled gently, 'but if you can't do any better than you've managed so far—ah, would you!'

As he spoke, Riordon swung round, gun in hand. Two little stabs of yellow flame spat out almost simultaneously. Two wicked zutts! of silenced automatics hit the air, and two bullets hummed. Devenish hurled himself sideways as Riordon's bullet whistled harmlessly past his head. Riordon tried to dodge, but Devenish's bullet scared across the back of his hand, making him drop the gun.

'You'll get more than that if you try being funny,' Devenish warned. 'So will you,' he added, as Rogers dropped his hand to his pocket. 'Throw your guns on the floor,' he ordered.

Three automatics clattered down, and Devenish chuckled.

'I will say one thing,' he admitted generously, 'you boys know how to take a hint. Now,' he said, eyeing the Hon. Marcus Riordon grimly, 'we've played enough. Where's Chester?'

Riordon was dabbing his hand with a handkerchief.

'You'll find him—when I send you to him,' he muttered.

Devenish tightened his lips, and his eyes were hard.

'I'll give you two minutes,' he said evenly, 'to tell me where Chester is. After that. . .'

He left the sentence in mid-air, but there was a nasty edge to his voice which made Riordon feel cold.

'Well?' queried Devenish, after a tense moment of silence, while the three men glared at him.

Riordon's lips twisted evilly.

'In two minutes,' he said, 'I can bring a dozen men out, Devenish.'

'How would they help *you?*' queried Devenish, with brutal meaning. 'One bullet. . .'

Again he left the sentence in mid-air, and again Riordon felt his blood running chill.

'You wouldn't dare to shoot me,' he muttered. 'They'd tear you to bits!'

'They might try,' murmured Devenish. 'You've had a good half of your two minutes, let me tell you.'

Riordon flinched.

'You daren't do it,' he repeated. 'You'd never get away. . .'

Devenish brought out his trump card, playing it easily, almost carelessly, but with his eyes gleaming.

'I would get away,' he said evenly. 'You've forgotten, my dear Marcus, that I never was the fool that I looked. Have you ever heard of the Bull Inn?'

Riordon's eyes flickered and narrowed. He said nothing.

'Because,' went on Devenish, 'at the Bull there are a number of seeming rustics who are *not* rustics. They are waiting until'—he consulted his wrist-watch with a flourish— 'until,' he repeated, 'seven forty-five. It is now seven thirty-five,' he added meaningly. 'Have you ever heard of the Wayside Garage?'

The name of the garage at which he had parked his car three days before had flashed into his mind as he spoke.

Riordon paled.

'You're lying!' he gasped.

'At the garage,' went on Devenish relentlessly, 'there are six men in a Daimler which has officially broken down. It will start up again at exactly seven forty-five, and the six men will come here. So you see,' he added with a delighted smile, 'I did not come alone, Marcus.'

It was bluff. Riordon might guess this, but he couldn't be certain, and Devenish's manner was very convincing.

Riordon felt a nasty sensation in the pit of his stomach. He was playing for high stakes, and had evolved a scheme which he had considered completely foolproof. He had not reckoned on the scheme going wrong.

For the first time, Riordon wished that he had not lured Devenish to Wharncliff Hall. But he stifled his fears as he took a step forwards, staring into Devenish's steely eyes.

'You're lying,' he said harshly.

'Now, now,' murmured Devenish. 'You really shouldn't...'

And then he stopped, his mouth open, his eyes filled with sudden horror.

Right across his words, shivering into the big hall in a blood-freezing echo, came a high-pitched cry of human agony! A man's voice, raised in the absolute height of physical suffering.

'My God!' breathed Devenish. 'If that's Chester...'

As he spoke, he moved. As he moved, the three men drew away from him. Rogers made one half-hearted effort to grab a gun from the floor, but before his fingers touched the butt, Devenish brought his gun down with tremendous force on the back of his head. The man gave one stifled groan and sank down in a senseless heap. Huggett, his eyes wide in terror, turned to run, but Devenish sent him flying against the stairs with a vicious right swing. Huggett's head cracked against the balustrade, and he sagged to the floor.

Devenish hardly noticed him—nor did Riordon.

The crook swung round as Devenish started his attack, and bolted up the stairs, from whence the cry had come.

Devenish, grim-lipped, trained his gun after him—but his fingers seemed to freeze on the trigger.

Once again that terrible cry rang out, high-pitched, long drawn, horrifying. And as its echoes died away, there came another scream—a woman's voice raised in terror.

# 15

## WHOSE BODY BURNED

Devenish went up the staircase more quickly than he had ever moved in his life. He could not be sure, but he judged that the cries came from a room leading from the landing, approached by one of the three doors which he had seen from the hall.

For the moment he forgot the Hon. Marcus, who had disappeared from sight.

He tried the handle of the first door. It opened easily, and he thrust it open, peering quickly into a large, well-furnished bedroom. But the room was empty. Devenish hurried along the landing to the second door. Again it opened at his touch.

But this time the room was not empty.

It was a bedroom, sumptuously furnished, but Devenish was not concerned with furniture. He stood for a moment, poised in the doorway and staring at the crumpled body of a woman in the middle of the floor.

She was lying full length, her arms wide-flung, her face turned upwards. Even as he saw her, Devenish knew that this was Lydia Crane. She was dressed in a vivid red afternoon gown, torn at the shoulder and revealing her creamy skin and firm, well-moulded flesh. But the thing which startled Devenish for a moment was the fact that her dress was badly burned at the hem.

He hurried across the room and bent over the woman, seeing an ugly bruise on her temple.

For a moment he wondered whether it would be best to revive her and force information from her.

Then he noticed a door leading from the bedroom. Devenish jumped across the floor towards it, and tried the handle. As he expected, it was locked.

The door was a stout one, and he knew that it would be useless to try and force it with his shoulder. He looked quickly round the room, and caught sight of a small, heavy oak table in one corner. Without hesitating he ran to it, lifted it from the floor with effortless ease, and carried it over his shoulder to the door. Then he stood for a moment, the table raised above him, his muscles flexed, the veins standing out like whipcord on his damp forehead. He drew in a deep breath, and smashed the table against the wooden panels.

The force of impact sent a thousand darts of pain along his arms and through his shoulders, but he hardly noticed them in his satisfaction as the door creaked, quivered beneath the onslaught, and shivered open.

He stepped across the threshold, frowning as he smelt a pungent burning.

Then his heart seemed to stop.

There was a thin haze of smoke in the room, and through it Devenish could see that a part of the room had been partitioned off with a brick-built wall in which was set one narrow, wooden door. The smoke came through the cracks in the frame of the door —and through the wood itself.

It did not take Devenish long to reason why.

Inside the bricked-off part of the room, a fire was raging. Already the door had been burned almost through, and the wood was charred in a dozen places, through which streams of smoke poured, thick and pungent. There must have been an inferno on the other side. And the thought filled Devenish with horror.

Was Chester in there?

He knew, even as he moved, that if he was, there was not the slightest chance of rescuing him. Even as he reached the door, there came a crash as part of the ceiling beyond thudded down. A panel of the door gave way at the same moment, falling to the floor in front of Devenish with a myriad of red-hot sparks and a fierce eddy of smoke which stung his eyes and caught in his nostrils.

He staggered back, coughing, gasping.

The flames, now that they had outlet, began to shoot through the broken panel, stretching yards across the room, fierce, blazing streamers of fire. The intensity of the fire scorched Devenish's hands and face as he jumped back.

Try as he might, there was no going into that inferno. Whoever was in it was burned beyond recognition by now, and past all human aid.

And, Devenish thought, his blood running cold, unless there was an efficient system of fire-fighting installed in Wharncliff Hall, it would not be long before the whole building was a mass of flames.

The thought spurred him into action. For a few moments he had been stunned at the possibility of Chester being burned to death, but now he realised that the only possible thing to do was to get Lydia Crane to safety. Then he must lose no time in searching through the house—providing he was allowed to search.

Hurriedly Devenish retraced his steps—but as he turned to pick up the crumpled body, he was, once again, frozen to temporary immobility—*the woman was not there!*

He pushed his hand through his hair, and his eyes were hard. Riordon and his men had been active, even in the few minutes at their disposal.

Patting the gun which rested reassuringly in his pocket, Devenish hurried on to the landing, and looked about him.

There was no one in sight, save the two gangsters, who were still lying in the hall below, Rogers near the fireplace, Huggett at the foot of the stairs.

But along the landing Devenish could see a second, narrower staircase, leading to the top floor of the Hall, and he decided to explore the upper regions first. The fire, if it took the hold that he expected, would rise quickly, and soon the upper rooms would be unbearable.

His search yielded him little.

One room on the top floor he recognised as Marion Dare's. There were several frocks and coats in a wardrobe, and a collection of toilet oddments on a dressing-table near the window, while one of the books in a small bookcase was signed across the flyleaf with her name.

Half a dozen other rooms revealed nothing, beyond the discovery that they had recently been occupied by the Riordons' male servants. A number of razors and a medley of dirty collars, shirts and socks were on one communal dressing-table, and a round dozen issues of sporting papers littered the chairs and the floors. None of the beds had been slept in, Devenish noticed, and he was mildly surprised. If, as was likely, some of the men were on night duty, they had not slept much that day.

He hurried through the last of the rooms, then retraced his steps.

No one accosted him as he ran down the second staircase into the hall. There was something about the hall, however, which puzzled him. It was different from when he had seen it, ten minutes before.

He whistled suddenly and scowled.

Huggett was still at the foot of the stairs. *But Rogers was missing!*

'Well, well, well!' muttered Devenish to himself. 'This is a house of surprises—and that reminds me!'

As he finished, he hurried up the stairs again, and closed all the doors leading from the first landing. The smoke from the fire was beginning to filter through into the hall, and once the flames took a hold, the banisters and furnishings of the landing and hall would be quickly in their grasp; by closing the doors, he kept them back for a few valuable minutes.

Downstairs again, he rapidly looked into the two rooms on the right and left of the hall. As he expected, they were empty.

That left only the kitchen quarters of the Hall, and the room beneath the staircase, for exploration. If Aubrey Chester was not there . . .

Devenish felt a clammy sensation at the back of his neck as he started the last search. Across his mind flashed a vivid picture of Diane Chester, waiting anxiously for news of her husband.

But he forgot his gloomy forebodings as he walked quickly along the passage running alongside the stairs, for as he moved, he saw the door beneath the staircase open a fraction of an inch!

Devenish jumped back against the wall.

Quietly, tensely, he crept towards the door. He could not see it now, but as he moved he heard it creaking faintly and he knew that it was being opened. With his gun held in front of him, he slid forward.

Then he let out a sudden heartfelt curse.

His right foot, barely off the ground, struck against the grinning jaws of a tiger-skin rug, sending the rug sliding across the floor. The crack of the impact echoed loudly through the silence, and a fraction of a second later the door banged tight.

Devenish dropped his caution and jumped forward, trying to kick the door open before it was locked, but he heard the key turn. For a moment he drew away, scowling at the solid oak in front of him.

Suddenly, he pointed his gun at the lock. Time, now, was vital. Whoever it was beyond might be able to give him information which he badly needed, but he would have to get at him—or them—quickly. Already the passage and hall were filling with smoke which went deep down into his lungs, parching his lips and mouth and burning his nostrils.

His finger touched the trigger. Once, twice, three times, bullets battered into the wood round the lock.

Then he hunched his shoulders and threw himself at the door. It sagged inwards, creaking noisily, and only by straining every muscle in his body did he stop himself from hurtling into the room.

As it was, he caught a glimpse of a man's strained face and staring eyes, a man who was hunched up against the far wall of the room.

'G-great Scott!' stammered Aubrey Chester. 'I-it's H-Hugh!'

'So,' said Hugh Devenish, five minutes later, 'the only people you've seen since you've been here are Marcus and the woman?'

'L-Lydia C-Crane,' agreed Aubrey Chester. 'She came in about ten minutes ago, Hugh, a-and left her b-bag. That's how I h-had the k-key.'

'The crack she had on the head made her forgetful,' muttered Devenish. 'It would have been nasty if she hadn't left the key and I hadn't happened along. This place,' he added, sniffing, 'is going to be a funeral pyre. Let's get out.'

The two men moved along the passage and made their way towards the front hall.

They had lost five minutes, but not all of them in talking. Chester, weakened by his confinement, had promptly dropped into a dead faint after he had stammered Devenish's name, and it was only between gasps, after Devenish had dosed him liberally with brandy from a small flask in his hip-pocket, that he had been able to give a brief sketch of his captivity.

Apart from a minimum of food and air, Aubrey had had little trouble. Whoever had uttered the cries which had sent Devenish pell-mell up the stairs, it had certainly not been him.

Chester grimaced when he saw Huggett's body.

'L-looks as th-though s-someone lost his t-temper,' he muttered, with a sidelong glance at his friend.

Devenish grunted, striding towards the front door.

'I did,' he said grimly, 'and I'm likely to do it again, so be careful. Open, darn you!' he broke off, tugging at the solid oak door. 'We don't. . .'

He stopped speaking, suddenly, as the door resisted his efforts to open it. Quickly he glanced up and down—the bolts were drawn, and the handle turned easily enough.

But the door refused to budge, even when both men tugged at it.

Chester went pale as he looked anxiously at his friend.

'I w-wonder w-what that means?'

Devenish scowled.

'I've got a nasty idea,' he commented grimly. 'We're in a bit of a fix, and don't you make any mistake about it.'

The door, he thought, must be electrically controlled. Before Riordon and his gang had left the Hall, they had locked it—and in all probability had locked every other door as well. If it was electrical control, he thought, both of them were in a corner which would take a lot of escaping. Unless, of course, they could get through the windows. Even electricity, however powerful, could not prevent them from breaking through a pane of glass.

'Better not touch them,' he advised, as Aubrey approached the big windows of the library, into which they had hurried.

He picked up a stiff-backed chair, and swung it forward, staring through the window into the grounds of Wharncliff Hall. The chair crashed through the glass, sending splinters flying in all directions. One of them cut Lord Aubrey Chester's cheek, but he hardly noticed it in his satisfaction.

'Th-thank h-heavens we w-won't be l-long now,' he said cheerfully. 'I-I. . .'

And then Devenish, peering into the grounds, saw something which made him hurl himself sideways, sending Chester staggering away at the same time. Not actually a movement, more a *suspicion* of a movement, in the dark shadows outside.

An instant later a bullet cracked through the window, stubbing its lead nose against the far wall. A second spat viciously over their heads, then a third.

Chester looked at his friend anxiously, his face pale.

'T-that's b-bad,' he muttered.

Devenish, keeping cautiously out of the line of fire, swore vividly.

'It's not only bad,' he grunted, 'it's heavy odds against us. We can't get out without being potted—I reckon Riordon's got a ring of his thugs round the house—and . . .'

He jerked his thumb over his shoulder as he went on, but there was no need to emphasize his meaning. Before he finished speaking, there came a tremendous crash above them, sending the pictures shivering on the walls, and a hundred books jumping in their shelves. A rumbling, cracking thunder followed.

The ceilings of the upstairs rooms had fallen, eaten by the flames. Soon the house would be a raging inferno.

And if they tried to escape, Riordon's men were waiting to shoot them.

Their blood went cold as they stared at each other.

# 16

## DEATH OF A CLUB MEMBER

After Hugh's hurried departure, Marion Dare forced herself to sit down and pick up the fashion magazine—but she made no pretence at reading it. Hugh's grim, set face seemed to hover in front of her as she leaned back, her eyes closed.

The Whitehall number she was to call if she heard nothing from Devenish by nine o'clock hummed in her mind insistently.

Twice in that ten minutes, Marion reached for the telephone. As often she drew back. He had said nine o'clock. She might do him more harm than good by calling before then.

She opened her eyes, and stood up, a little frown of anxiety on her face.

A moment later the front door bell rang.

According to custom, Pincher walked ponderously through the living-room, with a slight bow in Marion's direction, according to another, newer custom, his pugilist brother-in-law followed him favouring her with a blatant wink.

Marion smiled. Wiggings was a characteristic Cockney and there were times when his humour almost made her cry with laughter.

There was another little custom, too. Marion had seen it enacted, with much admiration for the thoroughness with which Devenish worked, and the efficiency with which his instructions were carried out.

Pincher looked out of the window, into Clarges Street, before going to the door, to satisfy himself that there was no one lurking near who might have ideas of raiding the flat.

Now, apparently satisfied, Pincher went into the hall and opened the front door. Marion heard Diane Chester's voice.

'Is Mr. Devenish in?' asked Diane.

'No, your ladyship,' said Pincher punctiliously, 'but Miss Dare is here. Would you care to see her?'

Marion stood up, pleased at the thought of a talk with Aubrey's wife. The two women had met twice, and had taken an immediate liking to each other.

Diane threw off her furs as she sank into a chair.

'Any news?' she asked anxiously.

Marion hesitated. Would it be wise to tell Diane of the message? She decided to compromise, and tell half of what Lydia Crane had written.

'Yes,' she said, watching the sudden light in Diane's eyes. 'It's—well, Hugh's gone down, to look round.'

'Wharncliff?' asked Diane, who knew part of the story.

'Yes—Aubrey's there.'

Diane closed her eyes.

'Thank heaven he's alive,' she murmured. 'Anything else?'

Marion shrugged her shoulders, worried and anxious.

'Only that I've to call a certain number if he's not back by nine.'

Diane leaned forward, patting the younger woman's arm encouragingly. She could now see the anxiety in Marion's eyes.

'If anyone can get through, Hugh can,' Diane said with an assurance that she did not altogether feel. 'He's . . .'

She broke off as the door bell rang again and Pincher made his dignified way to the window.

This time he was not so easily satisfied. He beckoned Wiggings, who stumped to the window cheerfully.

He saw, as Pincher saw, a long low-lying car twenty yards or so along the street, a heavily-built man in rough tweeds lounging against it, and two equally heavily-built men making their way towards No. 77a.

Pincher nodded his head slowly, thoughtfully. Wiggings spat on his palm.

'Looks like 'em,' he muttered. 'Shall we. . . ?'

He broke off abashed as he caught Pincher's reproving glance.

Marion's eyes sparkled.

'What is it?' she asked, with a hint of excitement in her voice.

Pincher turned to her, solemnly.

'I had not intended to alarm you, Madam, but. . .'

'Stow it!' said Wiggings bluffly 'Don't you worrit yerselves, me ladies. There's a coupla beaux on the dawstep what might turn nasty, but jus' let me get at 'em. I. . .'

Marion stood up quickly and hurried to the front door.

Diane, Wiggings and Pincher watched her as she peered through the letter-box.

It was an unusual letter-box, vertical instead of horizontal, and both surround and flap were made of a peculiar type of frosted glass. From the outside it looked solid enough but from the inside it was possible to get a clear, magnified view of all callers.

One man Marion did not recognise. He was thick-set, swarthy, with 'racketeer' written in his battered face, his cold, fishy eyes. He had his right hand in his coat pocket, and something bulged there. Marion guessed what it was.

But she recognised the second man, and her face hardened. He was tall and handsome, with heavily-lidded eyes. She had known him four years earlier as Samuel Benjamin Martin, director of Marritiband Development—the firm which had sent her to prison.

Marion turned away, joining the others silently, her face white.

'It's not safe to open the door,' she said huskily.

The harsh, insistent ringing of the door bell interrupted her. Martin and his companion were getting impatient.

Wiggings fidgeted, clenching his hands.

'Jus' let me 'ave one slam at 'em,' he pleaded. 'I won't 'urt 'em, reely.'

'We'd better telephone the police,' said Diane urgently.

Marion shook her head determinedly.

'I'll call the number Hugh gave me,' she said. 'Wiggings, you had better stay in the hall, in case they try to break through, and Pincher had better watch from the window.'

She went to the telephone, and within thirty seconds heard a quiet, rather sharp voice at the other end of the line, a voice which somehow gave her much more confidence than she had felt previously.

'I'm speaking from Hugh Devenish's flat,' she said quietly. 'Do you . . .'

'I understand quite well,' said Gordon Craigie.

'He asked me,' said Marion, losing no time, 'to mention Wharncliff.'

'Has he gone?'

'Yes—a quarter of an hour ago.'

'Alone?'

'Yes.'

'Do you know why?'

'Yes—Lord Chester is there.'

There was a brief silence at the other end of the wire, then Craigie's voice came again, reassuringly.

'All right, Miss Dare,' he said. 'I'll look after that. Are you all right?'

Marion wondered afterwards at the extent of Craigie's knowledge—although she did not then know him as Craigie—and at the calm confidence of his voice. She spoke quickly.

'No—at least, I don't think so. There are two men outside, and another with a car . . .'

'Do you recognise the men?'

'One of them—a man named Samuel Martin.'

Craigie muttered something inaudible, and there was an edge to his voice as he spoke again.

'For the love of heaven,' he said urgently, 'don't open your front door until you hear from the police. Put a barricade of furniture in the hall if necessary, and keep away from the windows. That's all.'

He replaced his receiver, and Marion did likewise, looking into Diane's anxious eyes with a slight, relieved smile.

'I think we shall be all right,' she said quietly.

It was, Fellowes afterwards told Craigie, a perfect example of co-operation between 'Z' Department and Scotland Yard. Within five seconds of speaking to Marion Dare, Craigie had sent urgent request for Flying Squad cars to go to the Clarges Street flat. Within ninety seconds, two power-ful police cars hummed out of the courtyard at Scotland Yard into Whitehall, and less than ten minutes later they appeared in Clarges Street, one at each end.

Warned by the Bleddon's Bank outrage, the police took no chances. As they drove past the waiting car, they sprayed it with gas, and the man in tweeds, now sitting in the driving seat, gave one short, strangled cough and slumped sideways, dead to the world. Then, walking quickly but quietly, two plain-clothed detectives went up to Devenish's flat; both men wore masks, making them look like denizens of some strange undiscovered world.

The first notion Martin had of trouble was a slight, barely noticeable hiss. He had been trying to force the door of the flat. He swung round, his hand dropping like lightning to his pocket, but before he could touch the trigger of his gun, gas billowed invisibly into his eyes, his nose, his mouth. For a moment he reared, clawing the air, then he too slumped down, his companion dropping across him.

'Keep away from the door for five minutes,' called one of the detectives, as he heard footsteps hurrying across the flat. 'Then open it—there's nothing to worry about.'

'So we've got Martin,' said Gordon Craigie, when he heard the result of the raid, a quarter of an hour later.

'Do you think you can make him talk?' asked the Chief Commissioner, who might be sceptical of the charges lev-elled against Sir Basil Riordon, but had no hesitation about dealing with gangsters in the salubrious neighbourhood of Clarges Street.

'You might not be able to,' returned Craigie, with a ghost of a chuckle, 'but I am.'

Robert Augustus Bruce, a large, humorous-faced, curly-headed man, whose connection with 'Z' Department had started some eighteen months before, arrived at the bar of the Carilon Club at five forty-five that evening.

At six o'clock two more 'Z' Department agents, Tobias and Timothy Arran, joined him.

Tobias and Timothy were twins, but there was little resemblance between them. Timothy was a lean, weary-looking man, medium tall, fair-haired, blue eyed. Tobias was the same height as his brother, but his hair and eyes were dark, his manner alert.

All three men were expecting instructions from Craigie.

At twenty past six a waiter informed Bruce that he was wanted on the telephone. The Arran brothers awaited his return with a mixture of anxiety and eagerness.

'Wonder what job he's got for us this time,' murmured Timothy over the rim of his tankard.

All at once there was a sudden, stifled cry from the reading-room of the club, freezing the gathering in the bar to temporary immobility. For a moment no one moved or spoke. Then a middle-aged man burst through the reading-room door, his eyes staring, his hands waving in frenzy.

'Get the police!' he bellowed. 'Don't stand there gaping . . . get the police! Meeson's been murdered!'

In the uproar which followed, Bruce, who had received his instructions from Craigie and had returned to the bar, slipped quietly through the club and into the street, closely followed by the Arrans. All three men realised that if they didn't leave then, and quickly, the police would be holding them for the inevitable inquiry.

Bruce turned to his two companions.

'The Chief said hurry,' he snapped. 'Do you know Wharncliff?'

The others nodded.

'Right,' said Bruce. 'Hugh Devenish paid the Riordons a visit this afternoon, and Craigie thinks he may need help. Keep on my tail.'

He stepped quickly into the grey Bentley pulled up at the kerb, and in the next moment the big car was disappearing down the street, closely followed by Tobias and Timothy Arran in their super-charged roadster.

# 17

# More Trouble at Wharncliff

The Hon. Marcus Riordon stood on the drive leading to Wharncliff Hall, watching the faint red glow spreading over the heavens above the burning house. Lydia Crane stood beside him.

There was no sign of Devenish or Aubrey Chester.

Riordon's face was twisted in an ugly grin as a tongue of flame shot suddenly from the roof of the Hall, vivid and yellow.

'They'll get too hot in a minute,' he muttered. 'If we can get Devenish out of the way we're all right.'

'There are others,' murmured Lydia Crane.

Riordon missed her sarcastic drawl.

'I can cope with the others,' he said, 'but Devenish is too dangerous. All I hope,' he went on, an undercurrent of anxiety in his voice, 'is that no one sees the fire from the village.'

Lydia laughed softly.

'Your nerves are getting bad,' she said. 'No one in the village ever looks this way—they don't like us well enough.'

Riordon glanced at her sharply.

'What the devil's the matter with you?' he demanded, with an edge to his voice.

Lydia smiled to herself in the gloom.

'I'm tired of all this,' she answered, sincerely enough. 'It's nerve-racking, Marcus—it's getting us both down. Why don't you finish it and get away?'

Riordon shrugged his shoulders.

'I can't just yet,' he muttered. 'The stakes are too high. Another day or two, though . . .'

'It's been that for weeks,' said Lydia Crane wearily. 'Killing, killing, killing! It's too dangerous, I tell you.'

'Stop that talk!' snarled Riordon. 'I've got enough to think about without you worrying me. God! Look at that!'

As he spoke, a sudden aura of yellow flame shot up above Wharncliff Hall. Vivid, awe-inspiring, the fire raged over the roof of the house—and Riordon, who had started the fire cunningly, knew that the only part of the building not affected by the flames was the front hall and the two large front rooms. In one place or the other Devenish and Chester were waiting—waiting!

Riordon had posted his men at fifty-yard intervals round the Hall, knowing that when the heat of the conflagration reached its limit the two men would make a sortie, preferring to risk a bullet than be burnt alive.

He reasoned accurately.

In the front hall of the big house Devenish and Chester were working like demons, clearing everything they could move as far away from the slowly encroaching flames as possible. They knew that there was only one chance of escape—rescue from outside—and although the odds were heavily against them they determined grimly to wait to the last possible moment before leaving the house.

They could not last much longer, they realised.

The heat was terrific—a dry, scorching heat, made worse by the voluminous clouds of smoke sweeping from the upstairs rooms and along the passage from the domestic quarters of the Hall. Rarely a minute passed without a rending crash from above, telling of crashing walls, fire-eaten ceilings. On the first landing the flames had gained a fierce hold, great tongues of fire stretching sometimes to within a few yards of the two men.

Devenish, stripped to his waist, sweat rolling down his blackened face, stopped working suddenly and wearily straightened his back.

'We'll have to make it soon,' he muttered hoarsely.

He turned round, his back to the door, and stared into the raging fire. Chester, his shirt blackened and scorched, his trousers torn jaggedly at the knee, showing a gleam of white flesh, stared at him.

The fire crackled and hissed above and about them, eating everything that came in its path. It was creeping now along the parquet-covered floor.

The air was stifling, hot, and thick. Every breath was an effort, every movement painful. Now and again something cracked in the flames like pistol-shot. Pieces of wood shot out, thudding against the walls and the door; once a great patch of plaster dropped from the ceiling, smashing into a thousand pieces, which rained over the two men like a shower of shrapnel.

'That's enough,' Devenish muttered grimly. 'Are we going out of the same window, or are we splitting up?'

'We'll s-stick to-g-gether,' Chester gasped. 'C-come on!'

The library was filling with flames and smoke as they hurried towards the broken window—another five minutes, they knew, would have made their escape from the Hall impossible.

As it was, they had one chance in a thousand of a getaway. In spite of the gloom outside—it was dark now—the fire would throw their figures up in sharp relief, plain targets for the gunmen who were waiting for them.

Devenish went first, crouching low as he climbed over the low window-sill, dropping down with a thud and laying full length on the ground. As Chester came after him, a bullet hummed over their heads into the fire-filled room.

Devenish crawled forward, pulling his automatic out of his pocket as he went. Aubrey had the smaller gun which had been strapped to Devenish's calf earlier in the day.

'They won't have it all their own way,' muttered Devenish. 'Look for the flame when they fire.'

Another bullet whined an inch or two over his head as he spoke and he felt the wind rustle his hair.

Devenish swore and touched the trigger of his gun. Forty yards away he had seen two little flashes of yellow flame. Behind the flashes was the gunman.

He waited for a third flash, then fired. His automatic sneezed, flame spurted. Forty yards away a man cursed with pain as a bullet tore into his thigh.

The shooting stopped, and Devenish realised that his shot had hit its mark. But the next instant it was taken up again from a clump of bushes fifty yards to the right, and more bullets whined over their heads, dangerously near.

Devenish gritted his teeth as he crawled on, moving towards the gap in the cordon of gunmen. If he could get the man behind the bush as well, there would be a hundred yards or more clear space—and a lot could happen over a hundred yards when the shooting was confined to automatics.

The thought was hardly in his mind when he saw another flash of yellow over a hundred yards away. A bullet thudded into the ground less than a foot from his nose, sending a little spray of dirt into his face, momentarily blinding him.

Revolver-fire wouldn't have carried that distance. Riordon's men must have rifles!

The next two minutes confirmed his worst fears. Instead of occasional shots, a regular fusillade of rifle-fire broke out and spurts of dirt and dust shot up all around them. A bullet scored across Devenish's forehead, leaving a thin trail of blood. Another pitted into Chester's forearm.

'All right?' queried Devenish anxiously.

'So-so,' muttered Chester. 'L-let's make for th-that c-clump of bushes, Hugh.'

A short clump of laurels stretched to their right, perhaps ten feet from end to end. They crawled towards it, a sudden wave of hope in their breasts.

Just as they reached it the hope was smashed.

Not five yards on the other side was another row of laurels—and suddenly the bushes seemed to blaze with fire. Not desultory shooting, this time, but regular, monotonous firing. Tappitty-tap-tap-tap, tap-tap-tap-tap-tap-tap . . .

'My God!' gasped Aubrey. 'M-machine g-guns! W-we're th-through, old son . . .'

Devenish muttered through his clenched teeth.

'If they get our range we are,' he said. 'Don't try shooting them,' he went on. 'They'll find us soon enough.'

For two terrible minutes the machine gun fire rattled through the night, ominous, death-dealing. Slowly, but with awful certainty, the range slewed round towards them. Little spurts of dust kicked up a foot from Aubrey's face as he crawled desperately, crab-fashion, to the right, fighting desperately to stave off the end in a faint hope for the millionth chance.

Then, with startling suddenness, stupefying the two men into absolute stillness, the millionth chance came!

High above the muttering of the firing and the whine of the wind came the roar of a powerful engine, opened full throttle. One engine—then, Devenish told himself with a tremendous sigh of relief—a second.

Two cars were racing along the drive to Wharncliff Hall—and they could only mean one thing. Rescue.

The din of the roaring engines was pierced, suddenly, with a shrill, high-pitched whistle, and as the whistle screamed, the men with the machine-gun stopped firing. From all over the grounds of Wharncliff Hall little shroudy figures rose up and scuttled madly towards the belt of trees nearly a mile away.

Chester scrambled to his knees. For the first time in his life he lost his stammer.

'They're on the run!' he cried. 'Pot 'em, Hugh—pot 'em, they're on the run!'

Devenish dragged his friend down.

'Pot 'em nothing!' he growled. 'If they think they're cornered, they'll fight like hell! I wonder who—good lord!' he broke off incredulously. 'Listen to that, Aubrey! '

They both listened with straining ears, a tremendous singing in their breasts. From the main road, distant but clear came the unmistakable sounds of rescue.

Robert Augustus Bruce, the Arrans, Hugh Devenish and Lord Aubrey Chester were sitting in, or lounging against,

Bruce's big Bentley. A hundred yards along the drive, a dozen or more firemen had surrounded the burning Hall, their hoses sending thin streams of water into the red-hot building.

'Lucky there's a river on the premises,' said Bruce.

'Luckier still that the fire-engines arrived,' frowned Devenish. 'You say you couldn't see the fire from the road, Bruce?'

'Not even a spark of it.'

'It's queer,' said Devenish. 'If you couldn't see it, it isn't likely anyone else could—unless someone happened to be in the fields, saw the trouble, and scooted for the nearest phone. Maybe the Bull people will know something.'

But the Bull people knew nothing. And even after the party had quenched their thirst, and the three cars were humming Londonwards, Devenish was still puzzled and worried. How had the Fire Brigade learned of the fire?

For Devenish had first seen the fire in the second-floor room at about seven-thirty. It must have been ten minutes after that, at the earliest, before the flames could have been noticed from the outside.

And at seven forty-five the Fire Brigade had already been warned and had started out. The nearest telephone to the Hall was twenty minutes' walk away, and the possibility of a passer-by—small enough, in any case—having seen the fire and sent the call could be ruled out. He couldn't have reached a telephone in time.

Someone who had known when the fire was started had sent that call.

# 18

# OUTRAGE AT A POLICE STATION

Station-Sergeant Billitter, of the Line Street station, was like the majority of his fellows—solid, safe, but essentially unimaginative.

At half past six on the evening of the fifteenth of September Billitter was advised by telephone that an ultra-dangerous criminal named Martin, with two equally dangerous associates, would be brought to Line Street within ten minutes and lodged there until further instructions came from the Yard. Martin was to be guarded second by second—he was not to have a fractional chance of escape or of killing himself.

Billitter believed that he was fully capable of carrying out these instructions, although when he saw Martin and the two gangsters he realised why the danger had been emphasised. He took the precaution of keeping the men handcuffed, even when they were behind bars, and detailed two young, quick-eyed constables to watch them.

Just after seven, a lean, keen-eyed young man, who introduced himself as chief clerk to the reputable firm of Redmond, Soames and Redmond, solicitors, acting on behalf of Samuel Martin, arrived.

He spoke pugnaciously.

'I suppose you're going to tell me I can't see my client?'

Billitter hesitated. He *had* been going to say just that, but now he was worried. He had had no definite instructions that Martin was not to see his solicitor.

Redmond, Soames and Redmond were no small firm, either. They had influence.

Billitter shrugged his shoulders and turned ponderously towards the cell.

Throughout the interview, which lasted less than five minutes, and consisted of the usual questions in such circumstances, Billitter as well as the two young constables saw everything and heard everything. Afterwards they all swore that the only time Rothman had touched Martin or had been near enough to touch him was when the two men had shaken hands.

Afterwards, too, a small red puncture was found in the palm of Martin's right hand. The crook was seen, ten minutes after Rothman had left, to stagger and crumple up as though shot from close quarters. His face distorted and one short, rasping gurgle echoed in his throat.

When the constables reached him he was a lifeless heap on the floor.

Devenish heard of the murder when he reached the office of 'Z' Department just after ten o'clock that night.

His eyes were tired and red-rimmed.

'Turn in early,' advised Craigie, tapping the bowl of his meerschaum in the fireplace—the two men sat in the armchairs opposite each other— 'and turn out late. There isn't much you can do that others can't,' he added, with a grimace. 'I'll put someone on Rickett's tail.'

Devenish grunted.

'I suppose Martin didn't say anything?' he asked.

'Nothing at all,' said Craigie.

'Anything turn up about Meeson?'

Craigie pulled a wry face and shook his head.

Meeson, a well-known, well-liked member of the Carilon Club, had been in the reading-room of that now notorious institution from five o'clock until six o'clock that afternoon. As often happened when the bar opened, the reading-room was practically deserted at six o'clock, and only Meeson and a middle-aged man who had been asleep were in the room where Carruthers had met his death.

Meeson had died in exactly the same way. He had been poisoned by *adenia,* injected with a hypodermic needle. The murderer had escaped from the room through the kitchen, which was near the reading-room; the two rooms were separated only by a narrow passage.

'No,' admitted Craigie, 'nothing turned up about Meeson. The Yard is looking into his recent investments, but there won't be much learned until the morning.'

'It was Rickett, of course?'

'I suppose so. Rickett was at the club this afternoon, but no one saw him after five-thirty—they assumed he was in his office. Heigh-ho!' Craigie heaved a deep breath, displaying more emotion than usual. 'We'll get to the bottom of it one of these days, Hugh. Meanwhile . . .'

'I'll go home and go to bed,' said Devenish, stifling a yawn.

The next morning he went to Gomshall Gardens, more spruce than ever in a suit of gleaming grey, and handed Mrs. Horace Birch the enlargements which a reputable firm had made of her family group.

Mr. Birch, he learned, had not been home for the past two days. His wife had heard nothing of him, but his business often kept him away from home unexpectedly and she was not perturbed.

Devenish next visited the villa of Mr. Honeybaum, where the maid told him what he half expected. Honeybaum, too, had not been home for the past forty-eight hours.

Would Mr. Octavius William Young, the fourth and last Marritabas director, be missing also? Hugh wondered. In a very thoughtful frame of mind, he turned his car in the direction of 'Fourways', Barnes.

A hundred yards from 'Fourways' an indolent looking young man was peering into the interior of a stationary Bentley; with him was a large, curly-headed, humorous-faced mechanic.

Devenish pulled up alongside the Bentley, ostensibly to offer assistance.

The mechanic greeted him fraternally.

'Any luck?' asked Devenish, lighting a cigarette.

The mechanic—who was also Robert Augustus Bruce—shook his head cheerfully. The indolent young man, yet another 'Z' Department agent, whom Devenish knew to be Dodo Trale, shook his head gloomily.

'Not a sound nor a sign,' he said, 'and I've been waiting in the hope of someone turning up with a gun for the last two hours.'

'Something'll happen all right,' Devenish said with certainty, 'and I don't think it'll be long.'

He broke off suddenly and stared upwards into the pale blue of the skies, which was broken in several places by large white clouds.

As they listened, Bruce and Trale realised what had attracted Devenish's attention.

Very low, barely audible even as they waited tensely, they heard the hum of an aeroplane.

For thirty seconds the dull throbbing of the engine continued, sounding almost directly above them and seeming to come from the centre of a broad patch of cloud which covered them and hung over 'Fourways'. Then the hum was replaced by a sudden, vicious roar, coming from a quickly opened throttle. The edge of the cloud seemed cleaved in two by a long, sharp-nosed silver streak, which swooped across the skies, dropping at a frightening angle as it went.

Trale's eyes widened. Bruce swore.

'Down!' he bellowed. 'Get down, for the love of Mike!'

As he spoke, the silver streak steadied for a fraction of a second, seeming to hover over the squat building which was owned by Mr. Octavius William Young. Then, in front of their staring eyes, the three men saw a small, black object loosen from the carriage of the plane, a swiftly falling shape like a long black pear.

It landed full on the roof of 'Fourways'; but before it reached the house the three watching men dropped flat on to the road behind the long body of the Bentley.

They did not see the sudden cloud of dust rise from 'Fourways', nor the vivid flash of yellow light which leapt outwards in an increasing circle. But they heard the tremendous crash of the detonation, the thunderous, deep-toned roar. Hardly had its echoes shivered through the air about them when there came a second explosion, sending the great Bentley quivering on its four wheels.

Heavy pieces of wood and iron flew above their heads.

Shrubs, trees and bricks hurtled about them, dropping within a hundred-yard radius of the doomed house, thudding, whining, splitting into a thousand fragments. Something thudded into the side of the Bentley, sending it lurching towards them, stopping again less than an inch from Bruce's flattened figure.

The air seemed to sway about them in great waves, like the sea tossed upwards and outwards by a depthcharge. The very ground shook and quivered and seemed to roar.

Then, slowly, the noise lessened. Above it, Devenish heard the hum of a fast disappearing plane.

He stood up, grimly.

'All right,' he muttered. 'Nothing else is coming over. And,' he added in a hard voice, 'you boys won't have to watch this house any longer.'

All three of them walked slowly towards the heap of rabble and ruins which had been 'Fourways'.

# 19

# MARCUS RIORDON GIVES ORDERS

There were two things in common between Horace Oswald Birch and Robert Elijah Honeybaum. Both were members of the London Stock Exchange. Both sailed very close to the wind.

Birch was a small rogue compared with his imposing associate, doing as he was told without question; Honeybaum occasionally raised difficulties, even with the Hon. Marcus Riordon. Honeybaum, with a crafty understanding of the laws, knew exactly how far it was possible to break them without being broken himself.

There was another important difference. Honeybaum was a director of a dozen little mushroom companies, all controlled by the Hon. Marcus Riordon; Birch was on Marritabas only. He had no idea of the immensity of the risk that he was taking. Honeybaum, however, had a very good idea, and reasoned that as the risk was great, so would his pickings be proportionately substantial.

On the morning of the bombing of 'Fourways', Birch and Honeybaum made a quick but comprehensive tour of the E.C. district of London, calling on numerous brokers and giving the same instructions.

The brokers were to sell every possible share in Marritabas, amongst other flotations, and turn the bills of exchange into cash. That cash was to be deposited at the Lombard Street branch of Bleddon's Bank before three o'clock.

Although every one of the brokers realised that the shares they would handle were practically worthless, they knew that nothing could be brought home to them. They sold the shares in bundles of ten to blocks of a thousand, secretly where possible, to prevent the bottom falling out of the market, and handed the cash over to Bleddon's, receiving for their share of profit a comparatively high commission.

Money poured into Bleddon's Bank that day in a continual stream. Not cheques, drafts, or bills, but hard cash. Of necessity, money poured out of the other big banks, but there was nothing unusual in a sudden run on treasury—and bank-notes. No report was made to the police, and the safe deposits and vaults of Bleddon's were filled to overflowing.

That, moreover, was not the only exceptional happening at the Lombard Street branch. Bleddon's was buying bullion. Gold was being delivered in van-loads to the vaults, and more gold was changing hands that day than had changed hands during the last three years.

The City, alive to the slightest element of the unusual, sent its most experienced scouts to learn the name of the customer—Bleddon's, of course, was buying for one of the bigger powers, probably European—but the scouts learned nothing. Under a cloak of extreme secrecy, the bullion was unloaded at the Lombard Street bank. Estimates started at a hundred thousand pounds' worth, and jumped, by midday, to a quarter of a million. At one o'clock the first load of gold came from the Continent, and was landed by air-liner at London Airport. With the third and fourth planes the estimates of Bleddon's purchases during that hectic—for the financial magnates—day leapt past the half million mark, and hovered towards the round million.

Apart from the one central activity, the City was stagnant. No one was willing to take risks until Bleddon's policy was revealed, or the sudden rush on gold was finished.

After midday, the first murmur ran through Hatton Garden that there was a heavy buying run on precious stones.

The precious stones market, of course, was not so generally known as the bullion market. Fewer brokers were concerned, but those few took early advantage of the favourable ruling prices. Diamonds and pearls ran up the ladder into boom figures, and there was a steady demand for the less important gems.

Some of the sales, as usual, were conducted in hard cash—the precious stones market normally dealt more in money than in bills. Other sales were completed with drafts and cheques on the Big Five Banks—and so carefully was the run managed that no one realised that sixty per cent of the commitments were lodged with Bleddon's Bank. Actually, the fact that Bleddon's credit was called on proved an added security. Bleddon's was as safe as the Bank of England.

Only two people knew that Bleddon's was actually trembling on the brink of insolvency. Riordon knew it—and Robert Elijah Honeybaum knew it.

After a busy day, in which he had flitted from office to office, Honeybaum slipped into the Lombard Street branch of Bleddon's and asked for the Hon. Marcus Riordon.

A harassed cashier, who had taken more money that day than in any month for years past, sent his name in to Sir Basil, who had spent the entire day in his late general manager's office. After a few moments Honeybaum was ushered into the great man's presence.

Riordon was sitting back in his chair, his eyes glittering with inward excitement, his jaw set hard. Honeybaum, who had heard rumours that the old man's day was over, felt suddenly convinced that it was Sir Basil, not the Hon. Marcus, who was behind the day's ramp.

'I haven't much time,' snapped Riordon. 'What do you want? Money?'

Honeybaum beamed.

'I have earned it, Sir Basil.'

Riordon's eyes glinted behind his thick-lensed glasses.

'I'll give you five thousand,' he said.

Honeybaum's eyes narrowed to mere slits. His voice took on a sharp edge.

'Ridiculous!' he snapped. 'If you had said fifty . . . ' And then he stopped. His mind seemed suddenly to freeze, for as he peered intently into the old man's eyes he seemed to look into two murderous, icy pools. In them he read death...

At six o'clock on the afternoon of the amazing gold and jewel rush in the City, the Hon. Marcus Riordon, short and tubby but unrecognisable with a cunning application of grease-paint and a small black moustache, drove slowly along the City Road towards the Bank, and thence into Lombard Street.

Beside him, Lydia Crane leaned luxuriously back in her sables, and watched the scurrying crowds with a faintly pitying smile.

She was bored, but beneath her boredom there was a tremor of excitement. If Riordon pulled off his coup, this would be her last day in England, the last of comparative captivity, the last of boredom.

The past few weeks, she told herself, had been dreary, but the past few days had been beyond words. The Hon. Marcus had been on tenterhooks as the day of his reckoning approached. He had refused, literally, to let her out of sight—except for a few hours during the day, when he knew where she was, and when she knew that any attempt to leave the flat in the Temple, which Riordon rented under the convenient name of Smith, would have been stopped by the two armed, tough, and forbidding gangsters on the premises.

Lydia Crane knew too much. Riordon was taking no chances with her. It was not, she realised, that he was afraid she would betray him to the police—she was too deeply involved in his crimes to do that. But Riordon was half fearful that Devenish would guess that Lydia Crane knew enough to make trouble—and Riordon had his own ideas on the method which 'Z' Department would take, if necessary, to obtain information.

The Hon. Marcus breathed more freely when he had his eyes on her, although once or twice he wished that he had left her in the flat that evening. There was just the possibility that she would be recognised, and it might lead to trouble.

Beyond that one small fear, however, the Hon. Marcus was feeling on top of the world. Everything had come off, although there had certainly been times during the past few days when Devenish had seemed likely to bring his plans tumbling about his head. But the danger was past. . ..

Riordon drove along complacently. In Lombard Street he saw a plain van drawn up outside Bleddon's ostensibly moving old papers from the Bank. Other vans had been there and others would be. Bleddon's, the police had been informed, was transferring these papers, the accumulation of years, to another branch. The opportunity for robbery, or worse, was considerable, and the police kept a strong and watchful guard on the vans as they drew up, were loaded with box after box, and moved off. There was going to be no opportunity for another successful hold-up.

And every box was filled with gold.

At six-thirty Riordon passed the head office of Bleddon's for the second time, and glanced upwards. As he stared, a man's dark, expressionless face appeared for a moment in a second-floor window.

Riordon grunted and accelerated. The car leapt forward.

'Is everything all right?' drawled Lydia Crane.

Riordon beat a red traffic light by a split second, and the car hummed towards the Mansion House.

'Yes,' he muttered. 'That was the last van.'

There was a hard gleam in his eyes, a flicker of triumph on his lips. The thing was done! All that remained was the getaway.

'Where now?' demanded his companion.

Riordon flashed a cunning smile.

'You'll know soon enough,' he muttered. 'I'm not taking any chances, my dear, with you or with anyone else.'

Lydia Crane laughed lightly, and dropped into a long, contemplative silence.

⚜ ⚜ ⚜

Riordon forgot her as he drove rapidly towards the open country, aiming first for Putney then Kingston. As he twisted the car between the traffic, he ran his mind over the few remaining things to be done.

There was little left, he thought with grim satisfaction. Even though Marritaba Tin Shares had nearly proved his undoing, the danger had been averted.

Marritabas, of course, had been a bad mistake—even a foolish one. They had brought in little more than a hundred thousand pounds—child's play compared with the bullion which had been removed in those vans which officially carried paper, and with the two cases of precious stones now safely in the boot of his own car.

When Carruthers, one of the easiest victims of the Riordon swindles, had been murdered, the first dangerspot had been removed.

Meeson, another victim of the ramp, had died a few days later. Both Meeson and Carruthers had grounds for *knowing* that Riordon was behind Marritabas.

Then there had been Macauly, the General Manager of Bleddon's Bank. Macauly had said, in a brief letter to Sir Basil, two days before his death, that he felt uneasy at the support which Bleddon's was giving to Marritaba Tins. Consequently Macauly had died. The raid on Bleddon's, as Devenish had reasoned, was only a cover for the murder. Until the gold-buying was over, the Hon. Marcus had been forced to keep Bleddon's credit at a high-water mark. If Macauly had been murdered without the camouflage of the hold-up there would have been a run on the Bank. Few countries would have risked selling their gold through Bleddon's while there had been the slightest question as to the security of Bleddon's credit.

There still remained Devenish, of course, and Marion Dare, but Riordon now felt that if Marion Dare had revealed anything of vital importance Devenish would have already acted on it. The only thing that remained to be done was to avoid Devenish—and it was only a matter of hours now before any effort he might make would be useless.

There had been several little things which had worried the Hon. Marcus Riordon. The failure of the attempts to kill Devenish, for instance: when he had been trapped at Wharncliff, and in the premature 'accident' with the Aston Martin which had been fitted with Devenish's number. Riordon still couldn't understand how that had misfired. It had been planned so carefully that failure should not have been possible. First, Devenish was to have been lured to Wharncliff. Then his car, with the unfortunate victim, was to have been discovered, both car and body burnt beyond recognition. Thus, Riordon had reasoned, there would have been no hue and cry for the agent of 'Z' Department.

There was another thing which still worried Riordon when he thought of it. He had heard and seen the fire engine which had raced to Wharncliff Hall, and, like Devenish, he could not understand how the brigade had received the call.

Yet another dangerous situation had arisen when Martin had been captured at the Clarges Street flat. But for the fact that Riordon had learned of the failure of the raid on the flat through a fourth member of the party who had been waiting nearby, he could never have got at Martin in time to prevent him from talking. But the fourth man had seen the police and had followed the police car to Line Street, telephoning Riordon very quickly afterwards. With the help of one of his many hirelings, the bogus clerk of Redmond, Soames and Redmond, Martin had been effectively silenced—and there was one less to share the proceeds of the coup which was going to stagger the City to its very foundations within the next forty-eight hours.

Then, thought Riordon, there had been Honeybaum—far too crafty an accomplice to have been left alive in England. But now Honeybaum was dead, his body locked in a vault in Bleddon's Bank—it would probably stay there for weeks.

There remained only Lydia Crane, Octavius William Young—or Rickett, and the thirty roughnecks and exlags who comprised the gang. Riordon did not worry about Horace Birch; the man had been a cat's-paw, and knew nothing worth knowing.

The further he drew from London the more the Hon. Marcus congratulated himself. The fact that all his hirelings were old lags—most of them with crimes which he had been able to hold over their heads, ensuring their compliance with his instructions—was a distinct advantage. Only fear could have held the gang together.

And so, Riordon thought again, there remained only the woman at his side and Rickett—and Marion Dare.

He was not afraid that either Lydia or Rickett would turn on him. Both were in his toils as deeply as they could be—both were as deeply implicated as he was himself.

For a while Lydia would be useful; for just as long, in fact, as it was necessary for him to keep in hiding. After that . . .

Riordon gave a queer, mirthless laugh. There had been a time, he reminded himself, when he thought that he would never get tired of Lydia. Now . . .

Lydia Crane turned her large eyes towards Riordon. She disliked the sound of that laugh.

The Hon. Marcus took a plump hand from the wheel and patted her knee reassuringly.

'It won't be long now, my dear,' he murmured. 'Another few hours. Do you feel like a drink?'

'I've never felt more like one.'

Riordon patted her knee again.

'We can spare five minutes,' he said. 'There's a pub just along the road—we'll pull up. You've been very good, my dear, very good.'

He laughed again, and he was still grinning at his thoughts when he pulled into the courtyard of the King's Head, an isolated public house two miles on the London side of Guildford.

While Lydia Crane drank a large gin and tonic in the bar, the Hon. Marcus Riordon hurried to a telephone in the passage outside. He spoke for ten minutes to a man at a hotel on the outskirts of Shoreham, Sussex; learned much to his satisfaction; and gave a series of orders which he knew would be obeyed to the last letter.

# 20

# Devenish Gets Going

When Hugh Devenish's Aston Martin hummed into Clarges Street half an hour after the bombing of 'Fourways', he noticed not one, but seven or eight solid, grim-faced, but apparently unoccupied men within earshot. None of them appeared to notice him, although he grinned at them all cheerily, feeling that Chief Commissioner William Fellowes did have some points after all.

He hurried up to his flat. Marion Dare stood up as he entered, and he held out his arms.

'If I tried for a year,' said Devenish. 'But. . .' He stepped back, his face suddenly serious— 'We haven't much time.'

Marion's eyes clouded.

'Is there any news?' she asked.

Devenish decided not to worry her with an account of the bombing.

'Yes and no.' He picked up the telephone and dialled Aubrey Chester's number. 'Hallo. That you, Aubrey? Hop round here when you can, will you? And bring Diane. I've got to go out for a bit, and Marion wants company.'

Aubrey promised they'd be round in less than an hour, and Devenish replaced the receiver.

'Now'—he took Marion's shoulders between his firm fingers— 'don't leave the flat until you hear from me. Not even if Aubrey suggests it, or Diane, or the whole police force—assuming the place isn't on fire,' he added optimistically. 'Got that?'

Marion nodded.

'Good girl!' said Devenish.

He said good-bye, but he could not tell her where he was going, nor why he felt in his bones that the affair of the Riordons was fast nearing its end.

Twenty minutes later he entered the room in Whitehall which he knew as 'Z' Department.

Gordon Craigie smiled a welcome.

'You've heard about the Barnes business?' Devenish asked, without preamble.

Craigie nodded.

'What do you think about it?'

'I think it's a case of burning their boats,' said Craigie.

Devenish lit a cigarette and blew a streamer of grey smoke across the room.

'So do I,' he admitted. 'And they wouldn't burn their boats if they wanted them again. Riordon's too crafty for that. . .'

'Which one?' asked Craigie.

Devenish scowled.

'I don't know—yet,' he admitted. 'But I will, before we're much older. Anyhow—Wharncliff has gone up in smoke, and so has "Fourways". The next hiding-place of the Hon. Marcus isn't likely to be so near home, I reckon.'

Craigie raised his eyebrows interrogatively.

'Where, then?'

Devenish laughed grimly.

'I'll wager a pound to a penny,' he offered, 'that Marcus won't be in England after tonight— if he slips through our fingers. But I've got an idea about that,' he added. 'Where's his yacht, Gordon?'

Craigie's eyes narrowed.

'So you think he'll make a getaway in *Madame X,* do you?' he murmured.

Devenish passed over the fact that his Chief was familiar with the name of the Hon. Marcus Riordon's supermodern yacht and nodded grimly.

Craigie fingered his chin.

'I've wondered that myself,' he admitted. 'The yacht's down at Shoreham.'

'So shall I be, soon,' grunted Devenish. 'And I shouldn't be surprised if it's not a big job. How many of the boys can you spare?'

Craigie tapped his fingers against the arm of his chair thoughtfully. There was a lot to be said for Devenish's reasoning. On the other hand, it was quite possible that the Hon. Marcus had already calculated that the authorities would be watching the yacht, and that he had made arrangements accordingly.

He said as much. Devenish nodded.

'I shouldn't be surprised,' he admitted, 'but I'll run down to Shoreham right away, Gordon, and see what there is to see. Meanwhile—any news from Wharncliff?'

Craigie shrugged.

'Nobody knows.'

Devenish lit a second cigarette at the stub of his first.

'I wonder whether it is Marcus behind it?' he muttered, echoing the thought which had been in Craigie's mind since the Chief had learned of the financier's sudden activity.

'I don't know,' said Craigie. 'I don't even know what the game is yet. But it's one or the other or both, and the game's big. And if Bleddon's is mixed up in it, there'll be hell to pay.'

'Bleddon's is mixed up in it all right,' said Devenish grimly. 'However—have you looked up that company business, yet?'

Craigie shook his head.

'It's a long job,' he pointed out. 'But Fellowes reckoned he'd have some news pretty soon. In fact. . .' he glanced at his watch— 'he should be getting in touch any minute.'

Chief Commissioner William Fellowes, it happened, was at that moment reading a series of facts and figures which lay in front of him on his desk at Scotland Yard.

On the previous day, 'Z' Department—through Craigie, but inspired in this instance by Hugh Devenish—had put through a request which had caused more heartburning and record searching at Companies House than there had been for years.

The company registers were searched, one by one, for companies, limited or registered, who were controlled in any way by one of four gentlemen—which gentlemen were known to Hugh Devenish as Birch, Honeybaum, Martin and Octavius William Young, alternatively Rickett.

William Fellowes learned, when he examined the report, that some seventy-six companies had been fortunate in having one or other of those four gentlemen on their boards. He also learned that each of the companies had failed, and failed badly.

It was a tremendously illuminating report, and Fellowes ungrudgingly admitted that it was due entirely to the efforts of Hugh Devenish. When Devenish had secured the photographs of Birch and Martin, and had proved the identity of Octavius Young—or proved it near enough—he had reported in due course to Craigie, and Craigie had passed the photographs on to the Yard. Thereafter a number of thorough and experienced policemen had combed the City of London for information about Birch, Young, Martin, and Honeybaum. Young and Martin, it had been conclusively discovered, had operated under several names, which names were now on the report in front of Fellowes.

Devenish was still sitting in Craigie's office when the Chief Commissioner telephoned—and twenty minutes later, called at the office in person. The three men commented briefly on the discoveries—and explicitly.

At a rough estimate, the seventy-six companies had defrauded a get-rich-quick public of close on two million pounds—Marritabas alone were responsible for seventy-five thousand.

Devenish looked quizzically across at Fellowes.

'And now,' he said mildly, 'Perhaps you'll agree that Riordon Senior isn't all the beautiful things you thought he was.'

Fellowes smiled ruefully.

'It certainly seems you may be right,' he admitted. 'Prove Sir Basil is behind it, and not Marcus, and I'll take you.'

'If he's not,' grunted Devenish, 'Marcus has made a dupe of his father for years. Because Bleddon's have backed up fifty of these blasted swindles. Laugh that one off.'

Craigie's dry voice broke in.

'Anyhow,' he said, 'we've got enough to pull in Marcus Riordon, as well as Honeybaum, Rickett, and Birch. Martin's dead, so we can't get anything from him.'

'There's the woman—Crane,' inserted Fellowes.

'Find her, find Marcus,' said Devenish shrewdly.

At three o'clock that afternoon Devenish telephoned Craigie from Shoreham Harbour and reported that there were signs of great activity on board Marcus Riordon's sumptuously equipped yacht. Not only was there a great stir on board *Madame X* but, so Devenish had learned by shrewd inquiry, enough provisions had been taken on to the yacht to keep the crew and a dozen passengers well looked-after for many weeks. *Madame X* was prepared for a long voyage.

Craigie was still not a hundred per cent certain that Devenish was playing the right hunch—on the other hand he realised that it was impossible to neglect the possibility of a getaway attempt in the yacht. After Devenish had rung off, he sat back in his chair, his brow furrowed, his fingers beating a light tattoo on his desk. Suddenly he made up his mind. Turning back to his telephone, he sent out a number of calls to various 'Z' Department agents—including Timothy and Tobias Arran, Robert Augustus Bruce, and Dodo Trale.

Within minutes of their having received Craigie's instructions, these agents were speeding towards Shoreham.

# 21

# AMAZING HAPPENING ON
# *MADAME X*

It would, reasoned Devenish, be useless to raid *Madame X* once Riordon and his hirelings were on board—unless perhaps he could persuade the Admiralty to lend a hand.

The latter plan, although feasible—for there was no limit to the power behind 'Z' Department—he viewed with disfavour. The Hon. Marcus, he fancied, would fight to the last; there was too heavy a penalty on his head for him to submit to capture. And Devenish had no desire to see *Madame X* with her precious—or so he hazarded—cargo and her scoundrelly crew blown to pieces.

As he watched the yacht, now at anchor a quarter of a mile from the shore, he reasoned that at least half a dozen of the crew would make a trip landwards during the afternoon. Riordon would be careful not to do anything which might catch the eye of possible watchers and create suspicion.

At half past three, after he had telephoned Craigie and arranged for reinforcements, Devenish amused himself at the bar of the Jolly Sailor, a pub on the promenade of Shoreham, which commanded a fine view of the yacht.

At four o'clock a thin-faced, sharp-eyed man entered the bar.

Devenish recognised him by the small carnation in his right lapel; he was a member of the Sussex C.I.D., and, as such, unknown to the man in the street but known well enough to one William Hearty, the landlord of the Jolly Sailor.

Hearty, a lean, lugubrious-faced longshoreman, saw the detective enter the saloon bar, and pulled a wry face. He had soft drinks at his bar, and had schemed permission from the justices to open for soft drinks only during otherwise forbidden hours and during the summer season. Hearty feared, with some cause, that rumour had winged its way to the police that his afternoon drinks were not always what they seemed.

He welcomed Tankerton, the detective, genially enough, however, and jerked his head towards the rear quarters of the pub.

Tankerton nodded. Devenish, toying with a lime-juice and soda, watched the two men disappear.

The interview terminated happily from Hearty's point of view. He cared less than a tuppenny cuss what the game was, providing his licence was all right.

Tankerton left the inn without a glance at Devenish, who, ten minutes later, looked interrogatively at Mr. William Hearty. Hearty nodded. Devenish, taking the first opportunity to move unobserved, slipped into the rear quarters of the Jolly Sailor and made a brief but thorough survey of the passage leading to the cellar beneath the inn.

When he reappeared, Hearty was serving three hefty, grim-visaged sailors, whose immaculate uniforms and hats bore the insignia *Madame X* in gold lettering, and who looked as though they had sailed the world many times, spending their leave in the toughest quarters of the toughest countries.

Each of the three members of the crew ordered lemonade, each received something stronger—which was the reason for Mr. Hearty's earlier fears. They had often received something stronger. . ..

But they had never been sold anything approaching the strength of the concoction which Mr. Hearty served to them on that afternoon.

In something under five minutes all three men were staring stupidly at their host, and as stupidly at the tall man leaning against the bar near them. There was a peculiar singing in their heads, as though they had been drinking for a very long time.

Devenish moved a little closer. The heaviest of the three, a swarthy, vicious-faced ruffian, bull-necked and broad-chested, pushed himself a yard away from the bar.

He glared at the landlord suspiciously.

'What the hell have you been doing?' he snarled, wincing as a sudden pain shot through his stomach. 'I reckon. . .'

What he reckoned was lost to the world.

As he moved forward threateningly, a man behind him slumped down in a heap on the floor. The barrelchested man swung round with a curse—but caught Devenish's first squarely on the chin. He teetered for a moment, then fell heavily across the inert body beside him. The third man, still partly in possession of his senses, made a desperate effort to get to the door, but he too met the full force of Devenish's fist, and joined his companions on the floor without a murmur.

Devenish paused for a moment to regain his breath, then he and the landlord between them manœuvred the three bodies over the counter and into the next room. Then, hauling the unconscious men like sacks of flour, they shifted them to the barrel-slide into the cellar.

Devenish went down the iron steps alongside the run, and William Hearty pushed the men, one by one, over the edge. They did not slide as easily as barrels, but they went down. Devenish prevented their heads from hitting the concrete floor, hauled them into a corner, and rejoined the landlord.

The two men went back to the bar, but they had no sooner straightened their clothes—Devenish running a hand over his dishevelled hair—than the swing-doors were flung open and a second party of the crew from *Madame X* called for a 'lemonade' apiece.

Another bull-necked individual lounged across the saloon to the bar, a yard ahead of his two companions. Devenish had seen him twice before—the last time unconscious at Wharncliff Hall. It was Rogers—the man whose unconscious body had been taken away while Devenish had been searching the top floor of the Riordons' country home.

For five breathless seconds Devenish thought that the game was going to be lost. Only the fact that he was looking studiously at a sporting print on the wall saved him from being recognised.

He flashed one warning glance at Hearty, who gave an almost imperceptible nod and placed a glass of whisky in front of Rogers.

Rogers tossed the drink down—and then he turned round. As he turned, his companions drained their glasses also— glasses which had been dexterously doped by William Hearty.

For a stupefied second Rogers stared at Devenish, his little eyes wide open, his mouth agape. Then, with a vicious oath, he dropped his hands to his pocket feeling for his gun.

Even as he touched the steel a queer, speckled mist filled his eyes, a peculiar popping noise punctured his ears. He staggered forward.

Devenish's voice came to him as though from a long way off.

'Sleep well,' murmured Devenish, 'sleep well.'

In less than a minute all three members of the second party of the *Madame X's* crew had slumped to the floor—as dead to the world as their three companions who had preceded them.

Ten minutes later Hearty and Devenish started stripping the clothes from the unconscious bodies.

Twenty minutes later several young men, who had apparently come to Shoreham for a spree, watched a dinghy-load of sailors pulling towards a vague, shapeless mass, the *Madame X,* now obscured by a slowmoving bank of mist.

These watchers had instructions to follow the dinghy after a given interval.

The dinghy reached the yacht, moving slowly, and handled with commendable skill by Devenish. A rope ladder dropped into the sea a few yards from the small boat. Someone on board the yacht bellowed a question, but Devenish ignored it as he hauled the ladder in.

One after the other the six sailors, each man an agent of 'Z' Department, clambered up the smooth white side of *Madame X,* Devenish in the lead, Tobias and Timothy Arran close behind. The whole prospect of success in the mad venture which had been humming in and out of Devenish's mind all day relied on two or three of them reaching the deck within a split second of each other.

As he climbed, swaying perilously against the side and frequently bracing his feet against the painted sheet-metal to steady himself, Devenish peered upwards.

Slowly, out of the damp, clinging mist which enshrouded the yacht, and gave him a much better chance of getting away with his attempt to take *Madame X* by storm, Devenish saw the burly figure of a man appear. He stood by the rope, and Devenish could see him craning his neck downwards to catch a better sight of the men who were coming on board.

Devenish's lips were set very tight as he reached the top of the ladder. On a level with his eyes he could see the rails round the deck, and a stout pair of sea-boots at the nether end of a burly sailor.

With a sudden heave he hauled himself on deck a yard away from the man, who was now peering at him with some misgivings. Luckily for Devenish the man was not sure of his suspicions, and hesitated before bellowing a warning to the rest of the crew.

As he hesitated Devenish hit him—then hit him again.

Unwinding a coil of cord from his waist and working with dexterous speed, he bound the now unconscious sailor's wrists and ankles.

A moment later Timothy Arran hauled himself on to the deck, closely followed by Tobias. Together the three men moved towards the first hatch. Their luck was in, for they had boarded the yacht from aft, not for'ard, and the peak-capped man on the bridge was looking away from them.

'Stick close,' Devenish murmured, 'and sway about as though you're a bit drunk. Are the others behind?'

He glanced back at the rope ladder, and at that moment Robert Bruce's head appeared.

Devenish beckoned, then went on.

As he and the Arrans reached the hatch, a sailor, thick set and with a knife scar running the length of one cheek, climbed up on deck. He saw Devenish and his mouth opened—and stayed open.

In Devenish's right hand was a wicked-looking automatic, and this, together with a certain grimness in his expression, told the sailor that silence was the best policy.

'Get him,' muttered Devenish to the Arrans.

As he spoke Timothy and Toby lunged forward.

They were on their man before he realised they had moved. He saw a pair of hands rush towards him in a kind of hazy uncertainty, then felt a queer, burning sensation in his eyes, his mouth, his nose. He gulped and staggered back, but Timothy Arran prevented him from falling, while Toby held a gas-spray in front of his face. With one gasp the man collapsed.

'We needn't tie him up,' murmured Devenish. 'It'll be more than a couple of hours before he gets over that dose.'

'How many do you reckon there are on board?' asked Toby, staring round him.

'Lord knows,' said Hugh. 'There's that cove on the bridge, and there's another for'ard, fiddling about with a paintbrush. We'll get them first.'

It happened just as Devenish had hoped.

The man on the bridge looked up sharply as he heard footsteps, saw Bruce's grim features, and shot his hand towards a lever, connecting, Bruce fancied, with the engine-room or the cabins. It didn't matter, he thought, lunging forward.

His fist caught the sailor square on the chin, and the man gasped, staggered back against the rails, and slid down. At the same time the man who was working on the paintwork of *Madame X* felt a sudden burning in his mouth and nose. He too dropped to the deck.

Toby Arran stuffed his gas-spray—which looked like an automatic pistol, but which was loaded with compressed-gas cartridges—into his side pocket and grimaced at Devenish, who was scanning the length and breadth of the yacht.

'I thought,' murmured Toby, with some sarcasm, 'that this was going to be a tough job, Hughie.'

Devenish grinned.

'It would have been,' he retorted, 'if you hadn't got me to show you how to do it properly. Round those hatches all of you—we'll get them one by one as they come up.'

Five times the same operation was repeated. As a man from below-deck climbed up he was met with a cloud of gas from the spray-gun.

'And then,' murmured Timothy Arran, as he stopped the third man from falling down the companionway, 'he just faded out. Well, well, well, Hughie! I never would have thought it. Steady—here comes another.'

After the fifth victim Devenish led four of the party below-deck. In spite of the complete success of his raid on *Madame X* he had a nasty feeling in the pit of his stomach, a feeling that all was not as well as it should be. From first to last the coup had been too easy. The members of the crew had invaded the Jolly Sailor conveniently in threes, and others had been dotted about the deck of the yacht just as conveniently. Too easy, thought Devenish uncomfortably. Easy enough to be suspicious.

With the Arrans and Dodo Trale in his wake, he went from cabin to cabin. All were empty.

'Not a sound nor a soul,' muttered Timothy Arran, as they entered the last cabin. 'This only leaves us with the engine-room and the bunk-rooms, Hugh. I. . .'

What he was about to say was lost in a sudden, urgent shout from above their heads. All four men went suddenly tense and still as the bellowing came again, thunderous, imperative.

'Get up top!' it boomed. 'Get up!—get up!'

Timothy Arran swung out of the cabin into the passage.

The others followed him, hurrying towards the hatch down which they had walked a few minutes before. Each of them was filled with a lurking sense that things had gone wrong, badly wrong. For they knew that the man who had shouted the warning was Robert Bruce—and they had recognised the unusual, almost frightening panic in his voice!

'He's stopped shouting,' muttered Devenish, grimfaced, as he reached the foot of the stairs. 'Go steady, you men— there's something nasty waiting for us.'

He crept up, his gun in front of him, pressing back against the wall as he moved. The others crawled behind him.

No sound came from the deck now. Robert Bruce's voice had stopped after that last urgent warning. There was nothing to indicate what had happened to him and to the sixth member of the boarding-party.

One thing was certain, however. There was trouble ahead; and trouble had overtaken the two men who had been left on deck to keep a look out. And Devenish felt dreadfully afraid that he had led his men into a trap.

Slowly he craned his neck and looked along the deck. At first he saw nothing, but as he crept higher he saw the figure of a man sprawling by the side of the deck, a man dressed in rough blue serge, his arms flung wide, his legs doubled up beneath him.

'My God!' muttered Devenish. 'Bob's caught a packet.'

The feeling of panic which had first started with that bellow from Bruce grew stronger. There was no sign of anyone lively enough to look dangerous, but Bruce was out—and from the ugly wound in the side of his face Devenish guessed that he had been shot from a short distance. Who had shot him?

The question hummed through Devenish's mind a dozen times as he climbed on to the deck. Before he moved towards the still body of Bruce he flung a muttered order to the three silent men behind him.

'Spread out,' he said. 'Don't get caught in a bunch.'

The words were hardly out of his mouth when something flew through the air and landed a yard or two in front of his feet. Devenish heard a little crack and tinkle of splintering glass—and then he saw a white vapour bursting from a broken phial.

Devenish jumped back with a cry of warning on his lips, but the gas worked quickly. It seemed to spread over the four men in a thin, white cloud, getting into their mouths and noses, deep into their lungs, biting, burning.

Their own method of attack had been used against them with a vengeance.

Devenish made one desperate effort to get back, away from the range of the poison, but he was too late. The gas filled his lungs until every gasping breath was torture, every movement agony. In front of him the deck seemed to rise up, a great white mass. Then, with a groan, he dropped down, slithering to the passage. And as he went the others dropped with him.

The boarding-party had failed.

# 22

# GORDON CRAIGIE IS ANXIOUS

Rickett, some time secretary of the Carilon Club and some time working as Mr. Octavius William Young, was sitting in a private room in the Grand Hotel, Shoreham, when the telephone buzzed and a voice announced that a Mr. Smith wished to see him.

It was nearing eight o'clock, and the sea mist, coupled with the early-September dusk, made the room a place of shadows. In spite of the gloom, however, Rickett did not switch on the light. He waited, sitting back in his easy chair for 'Mr. Smith', and his dark, saturnine face was fixed in an expression which suggested that he was very far from pleased.

A page-boy ushered the visitor into the room, and Rickett, looking towards the door, recognised the Hon. Marcus Riordon, but there was no welcome on his face.

Riordon hardly waited for the door to close behind the boy before he spoke. His voice was harsh, and a little high-pitched.

'Well, Rickett? Everything's still all right, is it? Nothing's gone wrong?'

Rickett shook his head and watched the Hon. Marcus pull up a chair and sit down.

'Everything has gone off perfectly,' he assured the other. 'Devenish and his crowd are on the yacht.'

'Have any trouble?' demanded Riordon, puffing a little with relief.

'No,' said Rickett. 'He boarded her well—just as you expected. I had two launches handy, and when Devenish had had time to get round the yacht I picked two of his men off.'

'Dead?'

'No—I don't think so. The big fellow—Bruce, I think—was badly hurt. The other man was just K.O.'d.'

'And Devenish?'

'I gassed him,' said Rickett, with a slow smile. 'Devenish and three of the others. There's nothing to worry about with them, Riordon.'

The Hon. Marcus nodded, tapping his fingers in a sharp tattoo against the edge of his chair. His eyes were very hard, and there was a triumphant glint in them.

Certainly, thought the Hon. Marcus, he had every reason to congratulate himself.

Devenish had fallen head-first into the trap which had been set for him. The exodus of bullion from London and the well, if discreetly, advertised activity on board *Madame X* had lured him and his men to Shoreham and on to the yacht.

For the first time, he, Riordon, had out-manœuvred the big agent of 'Z' Department. *Madame X* was not making a trip—the activity on board had been as spurious as some of the shares in Riordon's floated companies. The yacht had been a bait, and Devenish had swallowed it. While Devenish and his men were unconscious on board *Madame X,* Riordon would be off and away in another ship.

This other ship, the *S.S. Mario,* looked like a tramp. A large but dirty-looking cargo boat, she was anchored off Portsmouth Harbour, officially with trouble in her engine-room, to head off any suspicion. And her hold was full of gold.

Riordon stopped tapping on the chair and rubbed his plump hands together, very pleased with himself.

'That's fine!' he muttered. 'That's fine! Everything's loaded, I suppose?'

Rickett nodded.

A relief tug had steamed to the *Mario* ostensibly to see whether it could help the stranded tramp, actually to fill her hold with the bullion which had been brought, that afternoon, by Bleddon's. It had been done in the open, and no one suspected the real nature of the *Mario's* cargo. Nor did anyone suspect that the *Mario* was fitted with high-powered engines which would move her away from England, when she started, quicker than anything in England could move after her. The Hon. Marcus had spent a small fortune in fitting the tramp out; he knew the folly of neglecting anything which might cause delay when he needed a quick getaway.

'Yes,' said Rickett, speaking heavily, 'the *Mario's* loaded, and Devenish and his crowd are on *Madame X.* All we're waiting for, Riordon, is for you to get aboard—and the others.'

There was a peculiar bite in the tail of Rickett's sentence which made Riordon look up suspiciously.

'What the devil's the matter with you?' demanded the Hon. Marcus. 'What do you mean—the others?'

Rickett frowned. His dark eyes seemed to bore into Riordon's, and the Hon. Marcus felt, not for the first time, that there was a depth in Rickett which he could not fathom.

'I mean,' said Rickett, still heavily, 'all of them, Riordon. There's Honeybaum, there's your father, there's . . .'

'Who's running this show?' Riordon demanded thinly.

Rickett sneered, and his face was not pleasant to see. He leaned forward.

'I know where Honeybaum is, Riordon. I know where he is, and I don't like it.'

The room seemed full of tense, unspoken hostility. The two men stared at each other through the gloom; but it was Riordon's eyes which dropped first.

'Who told you about Honeybaum?' he muttered.

'Tomlinson did,' said Rickett evenly. 'He saw you shoot him and push him in the vault. . .'

Riordon jerked out of his chair suddenly, his eyes blazing.

'You interfering fool!' he snarled. 'What the hell has it got to do with you? Honeybaum was too dangerous—he would have sold out to the highest bidder.'

'He might have done, as things stood,' agreed Rickett, dangerously quiet. 'But not if you'd paid him well enough.'

Riordon glared at the other, his hands twitching at his sides.

'Who told you what I paid him?' he demanded.

Rickett laughed mirthlessly.

'Tomlinson. I had my doubts about you, Riordon, and I had Tomlinson watch you—and your father. He was outside the door when Honeybaum went to the bank for his money.'

There was a sudden gleam of fear in Riordon's eyes. He seemed suddenly to realise that quarrelling with Rickett was going to get him nowhere. It was too dangerous, doubly dangerous now that things were so near a climax. He lowered his voice and leaned back in his chair.

'Look here, Rickett,' he said, staring into the other's dark face, 'this won't get us anywhere. I put Honeybaum out of the way—he was too unreliable. Now there's just you and I and

Lydia Crane. Nearly a million each. Good God'—he banged one clenched fist into the palm of the other—'isn't that good enough for you? A million pounds and a clear getaway?'

Rickett's lips curled.

'It would be,' he said unpleasantly, 'if I was sure of getting it. But what's to stop you getting rid of me like you did Honeybaum?'

Riordon's features split into the mockery of a smile.

'Don't be absurd . . .' he waved a placating hand— 'you're in a different class from Honeybaum.'

'Perhaps. But what about your father?'

Again that furtive gleam of fear shone in the Hon. Marcus's eyes.

'Don't worry about him,' he muttered.

'But I do worry about him. He was at the Bank this afternoon—Tomlinson saw him up till four o'clock. But he didn't see him go out.'

The apprehension in Riordon's eyes changed to anger.

'That's about enough from you, Rickett. I've run this show from the start, and I'm going to finish it. If you want to back out now, get away while you're safe!'

For a few tense moments the two men eyed each other, Riordon red-eyed with fury, Rickett cooler but perturbed. It was Rickett who spoke first and now he seemed to realise that it was foolish to bait Riordon any more—then.

'All right' he said evenly. 'What's the next move?'

Riordon was too careful a student of human nature to gloat over his temporary victory. He answered Rickett's question quickly, and his words would have struck like a knife through Hugh Devenish had he been able to hear them.

'The next move is Marion Dare,' said Riordon slowly. He glanced at his watch. 'It's nearly half past eight now. She should be on her way.'

Rickett nodded.

'I hope she comes soon,' he said. 'The quicker we're moving, the better.'

Riordon nodded and lit a cigarette.

'She'll be here soon enough, don't you worry,' he said. Then his eyes narrowed. 'The only thing I'm not sure about,' he went on, 'is Devenish. If he gets away from the yacht it might be nasty.'

Rickett shrugged.

'Devenish will be unconscious for hours,' he said, 'with all those who went with him. The men he left on the shore have also been dealt with.'

'All of them?'

'Yes, all of them. I was watching while Devenish was at the Jolly Sailor, and I saw every man who spoke to him afterwards. You're getting nervous, Riordon. There's nothing to fear from the over-rated "Z" Department.'

Riordon grunted.

'All the same, I wish we'd managed to get hold of the Dare girl sooner. . .'

'Then why didn't you?'

'I had to wait,' he said. 'She's been guarded like the Crown Jewels all day. But we'll get her, don't you worry.'

Marion Dare knew that she had been guarded like the Crown Jewels all day—but she did not know that, to the Hon. Marcus Riordon, she was worth nearly as much as those jewels.

The Hon. Marcus was afraid of something she knew. And, ironically, it was not until it was too late that she remembered what it was.

It had been twelve months before the raid on Bleddon's Bank, that the Hon. Marcus and Sir Basil Riordon had bought the *S.S. Mario.* As secretary to Sir Basil, Marion had, despite their attempts at secrecy, learned of this purchase— had learned, too, of the highly skilled workmen who had worked for six months to turn the inside of the tramp into the most up-to-date ship afloat.

The only person, now, who knew anything about Marcus Riordon's connection with the *Mario,* was Marion Dare. And the Hon. Marcus knew that it was too dangerous a risk to let the girl remain in London for the first few weeks of his cruise. It was too dangerous, in fact, for her to be alive.

Riordon's plans were as cunning as they were thorough, but he dared not kill the girl until he had her on board.

Just after eight o'clock on the day of Devenish's illfated visit to Shoreham and the *Madame X,* Marion Dare was sitting in Devenish's flat with Diane and Aubrey Chester.

It had been, of necessity, a dull afternoon. Since Devenish had gone the only people they had seen were the police outside and inside the flat, a small army which Pincher bore with fortitude and the knowledge that they spelt safety.

A car drawing up outside the house made Marion look up.

'I wonder if it's Hugh.'

Aubrey walked across to the window and looked out. Marion followed him.

She saw a medium-tall man, with silver-grey hair and a hard, set face, step out of a closed saloon car.

'I-it's Bill,' grinned Aubrey informatively.

'Who's Bill?' demanded Marion.

'The Ch-chief of P-police, or whatever y-you like to c-call him,' stammered Aubrey. 'I w-wonder w-what he wants?'

Marion also wondered, and felt anxious. Every hour since Hugh had left the flat had dragged out interminably, and with each one she grew more frightened at the possibility of bad news.

The Chief Commissioner entered the room, and shook hands with Diane, whom he knew slightly. Aubrey introduced Marion. Fellowes's face relaxed a little.

'I wish I had met you under happier circumstances,' he said grimly.

'Not bad news, is it?' Marion whispered.

'It might be worse,' conceded Fellowes, obviously perturbed with his tidings. 'Devenish has been hurt—badly, but not, I think, fatally.'

'G-good Lord!' gasped Aubrey.

Diane touched Marion's arm gently as the younger woman's eyes widened.

'Where is he?' demanded Marion.

'At Shoreham,' said Fellowes, turning towards the door. 'I came along to fetch you myself, Miss Dare. The men outside wouldn't have let you go with anyone else.'

'Can I come?' asked Aubrey Chester, forgetting his stammer in the excess of emotion.

Fellowes shook his head.

'Sorry,' he said firmly. 'You'd better stay here, Chester.'

Something in that 'Chester' worried Aubrey. He had known the Chief Commissioner for a long time, and the familiar 'Aub' would have sounded better. Aubrey, however, forced himself to believe that Fellowes was badly hit by the news of Devenish's injury—there might even be a greater calamity, he realised. So he said nothing as Marion threw on a coat, picked up her bag and followed the Chief Commissioner down the stairs and into his waiting car.

But as the car slid towards Piccadilly, Aubrey turned worried eyes towards Diane.

'I d-don't like it,' he muttered. 'I d-don't like it a b-bit, Di.'

At half past eight that evening Gordon Craigie was the most worried man in England.

Since Devenish's telephone call early in the afternoon, Craigie had had no word at all from Shoreham. He sensed that something had gone wrong, badly wrong, in the attempt to board *Madame X,* but there was nothing now that he could do to remedy it. The yacht would be watched, of course, from the sea as well as from the shore. There were others besides the agents of 'Z' Department keeping in touch with the movements of the *Madame X.* But, according to the latest reports the yacht had not moved, and Craigie became convinced that the Hon. Marcus had some other means of escape.

Other things were worrying the Chief, too.

For over a year he had used one of the Riordons' accomplices as a stool-pigeon—paying for information which had been worth little enough, but had held promise of vital news to come.

That afternoon the man had telephoned Craigie to expect urgent information at any time. Since then no word had come. Craigie was certain he would have got in touch had it been possible. Now he felt that the Hon. Marcus had trapped the spy in his camp.

Yes, things were certainly black.

There was no news of the Hon. Marcus, of Sir Basil, or of Charles Rickett. All three had disappeared completely.

Craigie, knowing the resourcefulness of his adversaries, was beginning to be seriously afraid that they would get away with their haul.

He knew now why the gold had been bought, and why there had been an abnormal amount of cash trading on the markets that day. And he guessed the reason for the sudden boom in precious stones. Completely at a loss about Riordon's secret activities, he realised that the only thing that remained was to raid *Madame X* with a strong force of men.

Even in that he had little confidence. The complete silence of his agents was nerve-racking.

Some ten minutes after he had telephoned Scotland Yard, only to learn that the Chief Commissioner, William Fellowes, was not there, he had a further item of news which added to his fears.

Fellowes and his chauffeur had been found in a quiet corner of Regent's Park. Both men were unconscious when found, but had recovered, and had described how a car had run alongside them while moving through the park, and gas had been sprayed, by means of a gas-pistol, into their car. They had faded into unconsciousness, and the next thing they had known was a police sergeant and a doctor bending over them. Fellowes's car was missing.

Craigie was not surprised when on telephoning Devenish's flat, he learned that a bogus Chief Commissioner had called and taken Marion Dare away.

Craigie replaced his receiver quickly, then called the Home Secretary's number. After a brief consultation, he sent for his car and drove hurriedly towards Heston, where he could catch an aeroplane to take him to Shoreham.

Meanwhile a strong force of police and two fast-moving destroyers converged on the Hon. Marcus Riordon's luxurious yacht, the *Madame X*.

Almost at the same time, Marion Dare, unconscious after she had been drugged in the 'Chief Commissioner's' car, was carried into an aeroplane and flown towards Portsmouth, where the Hon. Marcus, Rickett and Lydia Crane were waiting to board the *Mario*.

About that time, too, Hugh Devenish, who had a notoriously strong constitution, was slowly recovering from the gas which had overcome him and his companions on the *Madame X.*

# 23

# HUGH DEVENISH HURRIES

'Sure you're all right?' demanded the police surgeon who had boarded the *Madame X* with two dozen men from a police launch now riding easily alongside.

Hugh Devenish nodded grimly.

'Quite sure,' he muttered. 'I'd give a hell of a lot to know where Riordon's gone, blast him.'

He turned away, a scowl puckering his forehead. On the deck in front of him, Robert Bruce, Dodo Trale, and the Arrans were also recovering. In the short time that they had had for talking, Bruce explained how a shot fired from a small boat alongside the yacht had stunned him, striking him slantwise on the temple. He had seen the boat just in time to shout the warning which had brought Devenish and the others on deck.

There was no use now for recriminations. Devenish's opinion of his ability had dropped a lot, but that helped little. The uncomfortable fact remained that the Hon. Marcus had completely outwitted the agents of 'Z' Department.

It was a hard knock—but soft in comparison with the one which waited for him when he reached shore.

Craigie reached the landing-stage as the police launch knocked against it. Devenish waved eagerly.

'How are things in London?' he demanded, as Craigie came up to him.

Even as he spoke he saw the grimness in his Chief's manner. Craigie hesitated a fraction of a second. Then:

'Go easy, Hugh,' he said quietly. 'We've lost Marion.'

For a moment Devenish stared at him without comprehension, as he repeated blankly:

'You've lost Marion?'

Craigie nodded. There was nothing more he could say.

Suddenly Devenish seemed to be looking a long way away from him. Craigie and the others had become part of a misty, unrecognisable mass.

'*My God!*' he muttered. 'And you don't know where she is? Where any of them are?'

Craigie shook his head mutely. The havoc which his news had created in Devenish was appalling. The crowd on the jetty seemed to sense it. Devenish stood there, the cynosure of all eyes, imposing, unmoving.

All at once he swung round, a fierce light in his eyes.

'He's left England,' Devenish muttered. 'I'll swear Riordon's left England . . .'

'Well?' interrogated Craigie.

Devenish jerked his thumb towards the *Madame X,* a vague blur on the grey waters of the sea.

'There are five men on there,' he muttered, between clenched teeth. 'If I can't get a squeak out of one of them, my name's not Devenish.'

Craigie grimaced.

'Go steady,' he cautioned.

'Don't be a ruddy fool!' snapped Devenish.

It took half an hour—the worst half-hour that Devenish had ever experienced Third degree. The words seemed to dance in his mind, a horrible fandango. There had never been such a third degree.

But he had to know—*he had to know.*

And then, suddenly, unable to control his emotions any longer, he muttered Marion's name.

For a split second the man in front of him seemed to go dead-still. Then, with a convulsive heave, he craned his bullet-head forward, and his eyes stared into Devenish's.

'That's it,' he croaked. *'Mario. Mario.* Riordon bought a tramp—the *Mario.*'

Devenish stood for a moment as though carved from stone. Then he uttered a short, harsh laugh, and cut through the cords which were stringing the men up to the ceiling. Bruce stopped the force of their fall as they dropped, half-conscious, to the floor.

Fifteen minutes later the ether was humming with the name of Riordon's cargo-ship. Portsmouth naval station picked up the message, and flashed a reply.

*S.S. Mario, laden machinery, cotton goods and tinware, bound for East Coast of Africa, weighed anchor off Portsmouth eight-fifty-five. Direction SSW.*

Gordon Craigie, hanging on to the telephone at the Jolly Sailor, had the message relayed, and passed it on to the half-frantic Devenish. Scotland Yard, acting on instructions received from the Home Secretary, contacted the Admiralty, and three destroyers, part of the Atlantic Fleet which was in the Portsmouth naval base, slid into the murky waters of the Channel and headed sou'-sou'-west in the *Mario's* wake.

It was not, the Home Secretary knew, a cut-and-dried matter of arresting Riordon and his accomplices. Something very much bigger was at stake.

The four or five million pounds which Riordon had obtained from Bleddon's Bank meant little. The Bank could stand the loss, and would, with care, make it up. But, thought the Home Secretary, if once Bleddon's credit was *publicly* doubted, there would be a tremendous rush on all branches of the bank. Every depositor would clamour for his money—and even Bleddon's would be able to pay little more than a ten per cent of the total call for ready cash.

Unless Riordon were caught, Bleddon's would be forced to close its doors.

Craigie, like his superiors, realised the tremendous gravity of the situation. Grim-lipped, he stood beside Devenish on the deck of H.M.S. *Dromore*, a destroyer with a limit speed of thirty-three knots, hoping against hope that their quarry had not taken too long a start. He guessed that the tramp's engines were tuned to immense speed.

The *Dromore* was swinging round towards Spithead when the first radio news of the *Mario* came through.

One of a dozen recce planes, which had left the base as soon as the news came through, reported a cargo-boat, forty-five miles west-sou'-west, cutting through the water at at least thirty-five knots. The ship carried only a fore and aft light.

The captain of the *Dromore*, a hard-bitten veteran, grimaced at Craigie and Devenish, and shrugged his shoulders.

'If the *Mario's* doing thirty-five knots now, I don't think anything we've got will catch her.'

Devenish peered through the darkness, vainly striving to see what he knew was not there. Since he had heard Craigie's 'We've lost Marion' the iron seemed to have entered his soul. Not for a moment had even the suspicion of a smile dispersed the thunderous cloud over his brow. He had been tense-limbed, strained, grey and gaunt with his fears of what might happen to the girl.

He had known, recently, a few days which would have been perfect but for the overhanging shadow of the Riordon affair. The few brief hours which he had had with Marion had been tempered by the knowledge that something might happen—to him. He had not worried about Marion's safety, feeling completely confident of the steps which had been taken to look after her.

And now his complacency had been blasted into smithereens. Marion was out there—with Marcus Riordon, crook and murderer.

Fears for her safety tortured Devenish. Doubts, half-frenzied visions, shot through his mind. His heart was as heavy as the seas through which the destroyer slid so rapidly.

He turned to the captain.

'And you don't think we can catch her?'

'Not unless she has trouble with her engines. Once she's away she can pretty well do what she pleases, and looking for a ship in the Atlantic is worse than the needle in the haystack.'

Devenish looked at the man for a moment, grim-faced. And then suddenly, the tension of his big body relaxed a little.

'We're about ten miles from Portsmouth, aren't we?'

The captain nodded.

'If a dozen of us put off in a motor-launch, we could be in Portsmouth in just over twenty minutes?'

The captain nodded again.

'Well, well, well!' drawled Devenish. 'A dozen of us could, and will. And,' he went on, his voice tense with excitement, 'we can hire enough speed-boats in Portsmouth to take us out to the *Mario* and back, before she's a hundred miles offshore. Can't we?'

Craigie snapped his fingers, as Devenish's plan struck home. The captain frowned.

'What good will speed-boats be?' he demanded.

Devenish almost smiled.

'Leave it to me,' he exhorted. 'Leave it right to me, and now be a good fellow and let us have a couple of your boys and a fast launch.'

Craigie broke in quietly.

'Let him go,' he said.

The captain shrugged his shoulders and rapped out an order. Devenish's idea seemed the shortest cut to suicide that he could conceive, but Craigie's agreement was tantamount to a command. Craigie was in full authority that night.

Two minutes later Hugh Devenish, both the Arrans, and six other agents of 'Z' Department, all of whom were on the *Dromore,* prepared for trouble, crowded into the lowered cutter.

And in Devenish's eyes there was a grim purpose.

In the cabin on the *S.S. Mario,* Marion Dare sat on a chair staring defiantly into the evil eyes of the Hon. Marcus Riordon.

No one else was with them. Rickett was on deck, and Lydia Crane was sleeping, or trying to sleep, in another cabin. Below deck, the *Mario* looked much more like a modern luxury yacht than a cargo-boat. Riordon had an eye to comfort as well as speed.

The past few hours had been a nightmare to Marion, but until now she had clung desperately to her faith in Devenish. Hugh would find a way of rescuing her. If no one else did, he would.

Now, however, she was beginning to realise the hopelessness of her plight. She had been on board the *Mario* for more than an hour. The ship was already many miles away from England, and every minute took her farther away from safety.

For the last half-hour Riordon had been with her, gloating, mocking. With the *Mario* racing away from England, Riordon's spirits were at high peak. Millions of pounds' worth of gold and jewels were on the ship, and there was nothing—nothing!—to stop him from escaping from the long arm of the law.

For a long time the Hon. Marcus had thought only of his campaign of crime. Everything was forgotten but that. Now the struggle was over—and he could appreciate other things.

Like, for instance, Marion Dare.

Something had seemed to snap inside Riordon when he had seen Marion, unconscious, with the shoulder of her dress torn during a struggle with her captors, lying in a bunk on the *Mario*. Compared with the dark exotic beauty of Lydia Crane, this girl was fresh, clean.

His eyes glinted, and he ran the tip of his tongue along his small pink lips.

'Of course,' he murmured, 'you don't like the idea, Marion. Not at first. But you'll get used to it, I can tell you.'

He stood up from his seat and leaned towards her. Unconsciously Marion crossed her hands in front of her breast.

'Keep away!' she whispered, almost inaudibly.

Riordon gave a harsh laugh.

'It will be better for you if you stop playing the fool,' he snapped. 'You don't know when you're well off. I'm rich—richer than your hero Devenish will ever be. You can have everything you want—why'—the small lips creased in a smile as he stretched his plump, hot hand out and rested his fingers on her shoulder— 'we can even get married, my dear. The captain can fix that for us in a few minutes.'

Marion drew back from his touch with a shudder.

'I'd rather kill myself,' she muttered, in a voice which she hardly recognised as her own.

Riordon stared down at her—and Marion thought, for one dreadful second, that he had lost control of his senses. His eyes were half closed, the breath came jerkily between his lips, hot, nauseating.

She turned her head.

Then, hardly realising what had happened, she heard Riordon give a sharp curse, and heard the swing of his body as he turned towards the door.

The *Mario*, driving through the water at over thirty-five knots, her engines working with smooth perfection, seemed to shudder from bow to keel. For a moment the ship half stopped.

Riordon flung the door open and disappeared into the passage outside. Marion, staring after him, realised suddenly that he had forgotten to lock it.

She stared at the door, her eyes wide open. Everything which Riordon had said and suggested crowded through her mind in a few seconds. His face seemed to loom up in front of her.

Very slowly, Marion went towards the door. She knew, then, that she would rather drown herself than stay on board.

And if she could once get on deck, the sea was waiting for her. Riordon would not take a chance of stopping the *Mario* to search for her in the darkness.

'Why have we stopped?' snapped Riordon.

Lorenson, the Dutch skipper of the *Mario,* granted and jerked his hairy hand towards the swirling mass of the sea.

'Motor-boat,' he rasped. 'Damn' fool was racing blind, mister. We rammed her.'

Riordon scowled. What was a motor-boat doing out as far from shore as this?

'How many in it?' he snapped.

Lorenson shrugged his great shoulders, but Rickett, who had been on the bridge, approached the couple with a mirthless grin.

'There are two in the water,' he said. 'One of the crew threw a life-line.'

'The ruddy fool!' snarled Riordon. 'We don't want anyone on here.'

Rickett shrugged his shoulders. Lorenson spat expressively over the side of the *Mario.*

Ten yards away from them a little group of seamen were gathered round a stanchion, watching the efforts of one of the men from the capsized boat. Riordon, cursing volubly, strode towards them, but as he went there was a sudden murmur of excitement.

Unable to restrain himself, Riordon looked over the side. Dimly in the darkness he saw the blur of a man's face, a man who was clambering up the rope thrown down by the sailor.

Arm over arm, the man hauled himself up, obviously little harmed by his sudden immersion. Riordon forced back a tirade of bad language. The crew were not in the secret of the *Mario's* cargo, and Riordon was wise enough to realise that he had best not antagonise them—yet. If he ordered the man from the wrecked motorboat to be thrown back, he knew that he would be asking for trouble.

Suddenly the man's head and shoulders appeared above the side of the ship. Helped by half a dozen sailors, he clambered on deck, and stood for a moment with the water running in streams from his clothes.

Riordon heard him speak, suddenly, urgently.

'There's another man down there!' the rescued man shouted. 'Why don't you lower a boat—he'll drown!'

The crowd round him, all Dutchmen or lascar sailors, guessed at his meaning. The first mate of the *Mario,* knowing that the owner might have other views, glanced over his shoulder as Riordon grew nearer.

Riordon's face was livid.

'Stop talking!' he bellowed at the new-comer. 'I'll have you thrown back if you kick up a row!'

And then, for the first time, he saw the man full-face, and his blood went cold.

'Trale!' he gasped. 'My God! Trale . . .'

Dodo Trale stepped back into the crowd of seamen. His right hand was in his coat pocket, and Riordon sensed that he was carrying a gun.

'Yes,' muttered Trale, knowing that the crew could not understand him, 'it's Trale, Marcus. And I've a gun in a water-proof cover. You can reckon you're for it. . .'

For a split second Riordon's face blanched. Then, with a shout of rage, he lunged forward. As he moved, Dodo Trale slipped behind a hefty seaman, sent one bullet thudding into the deck near Riordon's feet, and dodged back, taking cover behind one of the idle funnels of the *Mario.*

Lorenson bellowed a command in Dutch. The crew, suddenly realising that the man they had rescued could lead them into a nasty patch of trouble, split up, and made a half circle round the funnel. Slowly they moved towards it, with Riordon and Rickett in their midst, both holding automatics.

The life-line was still hanging overside, fastened to a stanchion. No one was near it. And Devenish, judging the state of affairs on deck, stopped treading water by the side of the *Mario,* where he had been swimming for the last ten minutes, grabbed the rope, and began to haul himself up.

There was a great surge of hope in Devenish's breast. He knew, of course, that his plan was still a long way from success, but half of it had succeeded, better even than he had dared to hope.

Guided by radio signals from the helicopters which had hovered above and some way beyond the ship, he had found the *Mario,* and reckoned that he could create a disturbance by letting his speed-boat—one of three cruising within easy distance—crash against the side. Before the boat crashed, Trale and he had dived overboard.

Thereafter, everything had gone perfectly. The crew had thrown the line over, and Trale had reached deck. Trale's job was now to keep the attention of Riordon and Rickett away from the stanchion to which the rope was tied.

Hand over hand, Devenish hauled himself up. As he reached the deck, he peered cautiously along it.

Ten yards away from it, a dozen men were crowding on Trale, who was hidden from sight.

With his teeth set hard, Devenish hauled himself on board. Then, bending low, he ran quietly but swiftly along the deck, taking his automatic from its water-proof sheath as he went.

More than anything else, he wanted to find Marion. Afterwards, if it were possible, he would do enough damage among the *Mario's* gleaming engines to slow her speed by half. But Marion first. . .

Devenish sped towards the first hatch, knowing that he might at any moment bang into a man coming from below but confident in his ability to use his gun quickly, noiselessly.

Above him dark clouds scudded across the skies. Beneath, he could hear the sea writhing and swirling against the sides of the *Mario*. To his right, the half crazed Riordon led the crew closer and closer to Dodo Trale, who was gradually manœuvring from barrier to barrier, so that he could make a leap over the side. Once in the sea, he would be safe from Riordon—and Trale's work was finished, now that he had kept attention away from the life-line hanging over the side of the ship.

Fifty yards away, two motor-boats were cruising noiselessly, waiting to pick up Devenish, or Trale, or Marion. Or all of them.

It was a gigantic gamble. Devenish knew that the slightest false move would send them all to perdition.

Silently, grim-faced, he reached the first hatch. As he drew near he caught the slightest sound of movement from below. Drawing back into the shadows, he waited, his forefinger on the trigger of his gun.

Slowly, furtively almost, the new-comer came up the steps. As the seconds flew by, Devenish felt his blood racing. Every moment was precious—vital!

Then, craning his head forward, he saw who it was.

Walking slowly, fearfully, Marion Dare reached the deck and looked quickly about her.

She knew that something had gone wrong with Riordon's plans, but she felt, now, that nothing could save her. If only she could get to the side and leap overboard! She felt that she could hope for nothing more.

And then, very softly, almost like the voice of a ghost, she heard her name called.

'Marion!' whispered Devenish hoarsely. 'Marion!'

Marion stopped dead-still, a tremendous surge of hope filling her breast. She turned her eyes towards the shadows, stumbling forward as she saw Hugh's big figure detach itself from the dark mass of the deck.

'Hugh!' she muttered. 'Hugh!'

Devenish's voice came urgent but soft.

'Don't say a word!' he ordered.

For a brief moment, he slid his arms round her. Then he released her, forcing himself to think quickly, to act quickly.

'We're nearly home,' he murmured. 'Get over to the side, darling, and lie full length on the deck. Can you swim?'

'Yes,' whispered Marion.

Hugh unfastened a life-buoy from the hatch and pushed it into her hands.

'If anyone sees you,' he muttered, 'throw that over and jump after it. Keep yourself moving in the water—it's cold, I can tell you! —and wait until you're picked up. Got that?'

Marion nodded, without question.

'But you?' she protested.

'I'll see you later,' he whispered. 'Get to the side, quickly, and if you have to jump, remember to keep moving in the water.'

Then, as silently as he had come, Devenish disappeared. Marion gave a little, anguished gasp, then turned towards the side.

Carris, the chief engineer of the *Mario,* was one of the hardest-bitten Scotsmen who had ever seen the inside of gaol. He knew as much as Lorenson, the skipper—the job they were on was dangerous, and if they were caught they were in for serious trouble.

He knew that he had the finest set of engines in the world, too, and he was careful not to drive them too hard. The *Mario* had averaged thirty-five knots since leaving harbour. Few ships afloat could beat that speed.

Knowing of the turmoil on deck, Carris watched his men working quietly, efficiently, as though there was nothing in the world but the great turbines. The furthest thought from Carris's mind was trouble.

But it came.

Ten yards away from him, a vast man, dripping wet from recent immersion in the sea, seemed to burst through the door leading from the crew's quarters. For a moment the man loomed there. In one hand he held a small round object covered in yellow oilskin; in the other, an automatic.

Carris opened his mouth, aghast. He moved forward.

The big man spoke, grimly, low-voiced.

'Get back,' he ordered, 'and tell your men to be flat.'

Carris hesitated. Before his eyes he saw what the big man was taking out of the yellow oilskin—gelignite!

'Get back!' repeated Devenish. 'I'll give you thirty seconds. Not a split second more.'

Carris swallowed hard and his face flushed. But he knew that the visitor meant just what he said.

Choked with rage, Carris rapped out an order in Dutch. Startled, his men turned round, saw Devenish, and dropped flat, covering their heads with their arms.

Devenish, tight-lipped, hurled the gelignite into the middle of the biggest of the three turbines. Then, without a glance behind him, he rushed away towards the deck.

For a few seconds only a little wisp of smoke bespoke the danger which hovered in the engine-room. Then, with a fiery splutter, the gelignite exploded. In the confined space it thundered and roared like a depth charge, a thousand pieces of steel raining through the air.

The great engines coughed and groaned. The *Mario* lurched sickeningly, then began to roll through the seas. She was helpless—a ship without power.

On deck, Riordon felt the shudder which ran through the vessel, felt a terrible, icy hand fasten round his heart.

He knew, and Rickett knew, that this was the end.

Sitting in the speed-boat which Timothy Arran was running in wide circles round the helpless *Mario,* Hugh Devenish sat with his right arm round Marion Dare's waist, her head resting lightly on his shoulder.

He had reached the deck safely, and Marion had been there waiting. Five minutes after they had leapt overboard, the Arrans' boat had picked them up.

A quarter of a mile away, on the other side of the *Mario,* Dodo Trale, his right arm hanging useless by his side, had been hauled on board Bruce's boat, The last act had been overwhelmingly 'Z' Department's.

Devenish eased Marion closer to him.

'So that's that,' he muttered. 'A nasty spell, but soon over. I wonder how long the *Dromore* will be?'

'The *Dromore?*' questioned Marion.

Devenish grinned.

'We thumbed a lift on a destroyer,' he said cheerfully. 'The captain wanted to know what use a speed-boat would be. We'll show him!'

Unashamedly, he kissed her. Timothy Arran, glancing round at that moment, groaned.

'Stow it,' he chided. 'You'll have the whole blooming navy watching soon. Look at that, boys and girls!'

A mile away, sparks flying from their funnels to make a deep, fiery glow against the dark background of the sky, H.M.S. *Dromore* and two of her sister ships raced towards the drifting *Mario*.

# 24

# DEVENISH TAKES THE COUNT

The last paragraphs of Gordon Craigie's report on the Bleddon's Bank Case read as unemotionally as Craigie habitually talked.

After the wrecking of the *Mario's* engines, H.M.S. *Dromore*, with her sister ships the *Hastings* and the *Bradford*, approached the *Mario* from north, west and south. One warning shot from the *Dromore*, falling across the *Mario's* bows, persuaded the Dutch captain of the *Mario* to surrender without causing trouble. Twenty men from each of the destroyers boarded the *Mario* and took control.

None of the *Mario's* crew resisted, but the Hon. Marcus Riordon endeavoured to leave the ship in a launch and fired his revolver, wounding two men. Rickett, Riordon's second-in-command, fired at his leader, wounding Riordon in both arms.

Riordon leapt overboard, and although the ship's boats searched for an hour, no trace of him was found.

Charles Rickett and Lydia Crane, Riordon's woman accomplice, were placed under arrest, and handed to the police authorities on arrival at Southampton. Similarly, Hans Lorenson, the captain of the *Mario*, was taken into custody.

'Charges against all three will be handled by the Chief Commissioner.'

'And very nice too,' grinned Hugh Devenish, sliding back in his arm-chair and pulling contentedly at his briar. 'Now tell me all about everything, Gordon.'

Craigie grinned responsively.

'The Hon Marcus,' he began, 'planned the whole scheme, from start to finish. Sir Basil took to dope—I think his son deliberately trapped him into taking cocaine—and was only active when fed with the stuff.

'Marcus, too, spent a lot of time making up to look like his father, believing that it would stand him in good stead before his plans were completed. And,' said Craigie with a wry grin, 'Lydia Crane was the only one who knew about his make-up—that was why he was afraid of her.'

'To make herself safe, the woman lodged a letter with another bank—the Central City—to be opened at her death. It would have told the police enough about the Hon. Marcus to have arrested him right away.'

'She was deeper than we thought,' grunted Devenish.

Craigie shrugged his shoulders.

'While we're talking about her,' he said, 'you'd better know that it was she who warned the Horsham Fire Station about the fire at Wharncliff, and also deliberately told Martin the wrong day for the Aston Martin trick . . . '

Devenish stirred.

'I owe her a lot for that,' he murmured.

'You do,' admitted Craigie. 'So do I. Unless she had talked, I couldn't have had all the information that I have. But to go back to Wharncliff . . . ' Craigie stuffed the bowl of his meerschaum thoughtfully—'you won't need telling that Marcus reckoned to get you there and leave you there. He started the fire in the partitioned room, after'—Craigie leaned forward a little, and his eyes were hard— '*after he'd trussed his father up and left him in the room.* Sir Basil was no further use to him, and he planned to get rid of you both at the same time. His plans went wrong when you managed to get out of the Hall—he'd reckoned to keep you inside with the shooting. When Bruce and the others came along, he was beaten—you can thank Marion for that,' Craigie added. Devenish smiled reflectively.

'I can thank her for a lot of things,' he said, 'past, present, and future. But you were saying . . . ?'

'So I was,' said Craigie. 'Now, Lydia Crane says she intended to warn you of the fire, and was waiting in the room while you were arguing with Marcus in the hall. When she realised that Sir Basil was being murdered, she tried to attract attention. It was Sir Basil's cries you heard first, then Lydia Crane's. One of Riordon's men, however, knocked her out—that's why you found her unconscious—and got the fire going properly.'

'Afterwards, while you were searching upstairs, Lydia was brought round and taken downstairs. She contrived to get into Aubrey Chester's prison, and purposely left her bag, with the keys. In other words,' Craigie said with a little frown, 'the woman did everything that she could, all through the affair, to prevent murder.'

'What'll happen to her?' demanded Devenish.

Craigie shrugged.

'I don't know—she'll probably get a few years' sentence for complicity in the swindle, not the murders. Anyhow, that's the limit of her part in the game, so far as we're concerned.'

'Now for Marcus again. After his father was dead, the Hon. Marcus adopted the best possible disguise—he pretended that he was Sir Basil. It was Marcus who was at the bank when the murder of Macauly was staged, and it was Marcus who was at Bleddon's on the last day, when the gold was bought over. It was touch and go, I can tell you, whether he got away with it, that time. He was recognised . . . '

Devenish widened his eyes.

'Who by?'

Craigie gave a slow smile.

'By one of the men he thought he had with him,' the Chief went on. 'Honeybaum . . .'

Devenish whistled.

'Then Honeybaum was . . . '

'An agent of "Z",' broke in Craigie quietly. 'I needed someone who was in touch with Riordon, and Honeybaum was easily bought over—he had an old grudge against Sir Basil, and wanted his own back.'

'From what I can gather, Marcus realised the game in time, and killed Honeybaum. If that hadn't happened, I should have known exactly what was going on, and would have stopped Marcus getting out of London. But I relied too much on Honeybaum.'

Devenish laughed ruefully, and crossed his legs.

'So Honeybaum was the real spy, and I was only keeping Riordon off the scent. Is that it?'

Craigie nodded.

'In a way,' he admitted. 'On the other hand, you discovered a lot of things that even Honeybaum didn't know. He didn't know who Marcus's chief men were, for instance. You found Rickett and Martin—Honeybaum couldn't help there.'

Devenish chuckled.

'All right,' he said, 'I'll take it lying down. Next please!'

Craigie tapped the bowl of his pipe on the hearth.

'There isn't a great deal more,' he said. 'Marcus blew up "Fourways" more for effect than with any purpose—it kept us busy while he was working his gold rush. The same with *Madame X*—she was refuelled and provisioned as a blind.'

'I don't know where Marcus was making for on the *Mario*. Nobody does, and it doesn't matter a hang. He bought the ship, and paid Lorenson well to do just as he was told, and that's all we know.'

Craigie stopped for a minute and poured out two large whiskies. Devenish stretched out a hand.

'Thanks. I needed that. You know, Gordon, we really got out of it darned well. Ninety per cent luck, and . . .'

'I know all about that,' interjected Craigie, with a dry grin. 'Ninety per cent Devenish and ten per cent luck is more the way I reckon it, Hugh.'

Devenish waved his hand airily.

'Don't forget the other boys,' he chided. 'Dodo Trale caught a whale of a cold after his second dip. He's confined to his flat, and I left the Arrans and Bob Bruce with him a couple of hours ago.'

'Making merry?' grinned Craigie.

'I think they called it beer,' said Devenish innocently. 'However . . . '

He moved his great frame out of his chair and looked thoughtfully at a clock on the mantelpiece. It was nearing three o'clock, and Devenish had a date.

'Talking of Marion,' said Craigie, with a sudden twinkle in his eyes, 'I . . . '

'Were we?' murmured Hugh blandly.

'Near enough,' said Craigie. 'Well—you'll hardly need telling, Hugh, that the theft that sent her to gaol for a year was a put-up job. She happened to work for the Marritiband Development Company, and knew something of Marcus's activities. He wanted—or his father wanted—a capable secretary who could be forced to keep quiet, and the robbery was staged. Tough on her, old son.'

Devenish nodded, but there was a grin at the corners of his lips.

'I knew there was something you could give us for a present,' he murmured. 'Fix that darned silly thing called a free pardon without a stain on her character, will you?'

Craigie cocked an inquiring eye.

'Yes,' he said. 'When do you want it?'

'Please yourself,' beamed Devenish. 'We're getting married at ten o'clock tomorrow morning, so I don't suppose it'll be ready by then. However . . . '

'That's good hearing,' said Craigie, with sincerity. 'Here's luck, Hugh . . . '

'Thanks,' grinned Devenish, reaching for his coat. 'Keep the good work going while I'm gone.'

The two men shook hands, and Craigie walked to the door with Devenish. After he had left, Craigie sat for a while in his chair, staring into the embers of the fire.

The thing was finished now. Riordon had killed himself. Rickett would almost certainly be hanged—unless he had earned a reprieve by stopping Riordon's shooting on the *Mario*—and Lydia Crane would get a comparatively light sentence for her part in the swindle. A dozen or more of Riordon's hirelings had been caught fleeing the country, and some of them would hang for Macauly's murder and Sir Basil's. Yes, it was over.

Craigie smiled, a little wearily, to himself. It was hard work, the running of 'Z' Department, and now Devenish was out of it—no married men were used by Craigie. One by one his best men had gone.

Craigie sighed, and leaned back in his chair. His mind began to work, slowly, on other, lesser activities of 'Z'.

'No, I don't,' said Hugh Devenish emphatically. 'Nor does Marion. We don't want anyone to see us off, Aubrey, my son. You go and say pretty things to Diane.'

Aubrey Chester smiled. His wife hugged Marion for a moment, and wished her God-speed.

And then Pincher, late for the first time in his life, drove up at the kerb outside the registry office, and made a dignified exit from the Aston Martin, a fresh painted, resplendent Aston Martin. Equally dignified, he ushered Marion into her seat, and closed the door after Devenish.

Together, he, Aubrey and Diane watched the car merging into the stream of traffic.

They gazed after it long after it had disappeared. And then Aubrey linked his arm fraternally in Pincher's.

'C-come and h-have a d-drink,' he stammered. 'Y-you'll n-need it, now y-you've got a f-family.'

# Death Round the Corner

### John Creasey

# PROLOGUE

Iɴ the Spring of 1930 the hotels of London were full to overflowing, peopled by a host of distinguished gentlemen from all corners of the world, with their secretaries, legal advisers, personal servants and, with a few exceptions, their wives. Those people whose memories take them back to that year will remember the influx, and will remember the cause of it. The World Economic Conference was widely reported in the daily papers, some organs of which poured ridicule and derision over the object of the Conference, while other and more sober journals helped with encouragement and a good Press.

No sane man could have failed to support the object, but many, while regretting the biting leaders in some of the yellowest of the Yellow Press, could only foresee failure. Failure came, for in 1930 the world was not ready for a united effort to combat the problems confronting it. The prosperity of some countries compared with the poverty of others so favourably that idealists claimed the prosperity should be and could be shared equally, but only the unhappy and parlous Powers agreed. The failure, foreseen by many,

regretted by most but heralded as a triumph for common
sense (or insularity) by those papers which had viewed the
Conference as impracticable, and which had launched a
vitriolic campaign against it from its inception, was hidden
in a smoke-screen of words; a month after their descent on
the Metropolis, the economists and their advisers made
their way back to their own countries wiser but sadder men.
Prosperity was still a national, not an international, consid-
eration. War was too costly, but Power would still fight Power
on economic grounds, and fight until the weakest nations
were no more than semi-independent.

No one had watched the Conference more eagerly than a
gentleman who for some time had been increasing his mon-
etary power in England and overseas. Mr. Leopold Gorman
was a shrewd man. Some years before he had become
obsessed with an idea, the fruition of which could not be
contrived by himself alone, but which was possible if he had
the help which he needed from powerful enough sources.
In the World Economic Conference Leopold Gorman saw
a way of finding this support. He spent a great deal of time
at the meetings, suffering the rendering of each and every
speech in five different languages, intent only on picking
his men.

The first qualification in such men was strong antipathy
towards the subject under discussion—the more equal distribution of wealth throughout the world. Secondly, their
standard of economic morals must be low. Thirdly, they
must be content to leave the managing of the scheme which
Gorman had in mind to him, without question. It was in
his search for the third qualification where Gorman found
most difficulty, but one evening in May, ten days after the

wind-up of the Conference, he met five men, all of different nationalities, all powerful financiers or industrialists, whom he considered would meet his requirements. He did not say so, but if any one of them had shown reluctance to fall in with his scheme, that one would have been dead within an hour of leaving his Park Place house. Having once broached his idea, Gorman dared not risk the chance of it becoming public knowledge.

But Leopold Gorman had chosen his men well. None of them turned a hair after they had heard him talk. Holstein, the German iron and steel magnate, and Yushimuro, the Japanese cotton dictator, were only lukewarm in their reception of the proposition, but it was more native caution and doubt as to the eventual success which would be met than moral reluctance which prevented them from being enthusiastic. Higson, the American motor and aeroplane king, was openly jubilant, and Miccowiski the Russian was as keen (although Gorman had not doubted his ability to persuade the Soviet of the advantages of working with him). Leugens the Dane, whom Gorman had selected because of his worldwide shipping influence and his virtual control of food exports from Europe to tropical countries, spoke first after Gorman had stopped talking and while the other four magnates were mentally digesting the Englishman's strong meat.

"Five of us are not enough," said Leugens. "We want five—even more—in every country."

"We shall get them," said Gorman, "or, what is better, we shall buy their interests in their own countries."

"That will mean big money," grunted Holstein.

"That," said Leopold Gorman blandly, "is why I did not attempt to handle the proposition entirely by myself, gentlemen. We six together are rich enough to make the scheme successful—providing, once we have started, we do not back out."

"How long will you give us to make a decision?" demanded Yushimuro.

Gorman eyed the Japanese thoughtfully.

"Will twenty-four hours be enough?" he asked.

"More than enough," grunted Higson. "I say yes, and I don't need to think about it."

"Me too," said Miccowiski.

"You?" Gorman looked at Holstein.

The German hesitated.

"How are we to know," he demanded, "that we can rely on you, Mr. Gorman?"

"That is not important." Gorman shrugged his shoulders impatiently. "We can discuss ways and means of making each one of us secure against any possible neglect on my part or yours. In principle you are with us?"

*"Ja."* Holstein lapsed into his native tongue unconsciously.

"Leugens?" Gorman looked at the Dane.

"Yes," said Leugens slowly.

Gorman turned again to Yushimuro.

"Do you still want twenty-four hours?" he asked.

The Jap shook his head suddenly.

"No. I will be with you," he said.

The smile on Leopold Gorman's face betrayed little of the triumph which he felt.

"Gentlemen," he said, "we shall do what the Economic Conference failed to do. We shall secure the more equal distribution of prosperity—amongst ourselves. Shall we dine, gentlemen?"

His five visitors laughed at his joke, and said that they would dine.

In the early Spring of 1935, Leopold Gorman told himself that the plans which he and his five backers had made were near maturity. By the end of the year he anticipated complete success, and that without creating a suspicion of his plans in the mind of any member of the English Government, or, for that matter, of anyone but those who were directly interested.

There had been throughout those five years only one man who had caused Leopold Gorman anxiety. That one man was the Chief of the British Intelligence, Gordon Craigie. Craigie numbered some of the most brilliant Intelligence men in the world amongst his agents, and Leopold Gorman told himself that his safest policy to draw Craigie's teeth was to kill his men. One by one, Gordon Craigie's best agents "disappeared", but that was the way of things in the Intelligence, and the Chief knew no more than that more men than usual failed to return after he had sent them on various missions.

It was in the May of 1935 that Leopold Gorman, completely satisfied with the way his plans had worked, decided that the next man on his list would be one Tony Beresford. It was about the same time that Gordon Craigie decided that Leopold Gorman needed even closer watching than he had had in the past, and that the only man he could trust with the job was the same Beresford. The Devil and Destiny laughed at their joke.

# Love John Creasey?

## Get your next classic Creasey thrillers for FREE

If you sign up today, you'll get all of these benefits:

1. The John Creasey Starter Library - Complimentary ebook copies of THE DEATH MISER and REDHEAD (usual price £5.98)

2. Details of the new editions of his classic novels and the chance to get copies in advance of publication, and

3. The chance to win exclusive prizes in regular competitions.

Interested? It takes less than a minute to sign up. You can get the novels and your first exclusive newsletter by visiting www.johncreaseybooks.com

33107763R00123

Printed in Great Britain
by Amazon